ALIBI
The Damien Palmer Investigations
Book 1

Stuart Holland

ALIBI
The Damien Palmer Investigations
Book 1

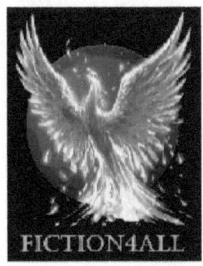

Chapter 1

The mid-October evening brought with it a cool chill as the wind played mischievously with the leaves that had already fallen onto the pavement and street. It was a grey evening, the cloud cover having progressively become lower as the afternoon passed. The woman, who was in her early thirties, walked briskly down the street her footsteps stirring the leaves on the path. She wore a scarf that almost covered her short blond hair. The grey coat that provided protection from the chill and her calf length boots made it impossible for any onlooker to guess at her ethnic origin. She walked briskly, with the air of someone who was in a hurry but unsure of where she was going.

In a moment she reached the end of the road. For a few seconds she paused as if wondering which way to turn. She looked behind her and observed the number on the nearest house. Fumbling for the tenth time in as many minutes in her coat pocket she retrieved a small white card. On it was inscribed a name, D.W. Palmer, his profession, and the address for which she was looking. She scrutinised it as if it were the first time she had read the inscription, when in reality she knew every detail by heart. This time she held on to the card as she turned left and continued her brisk stroll. She passed five dwellings, each almost identical to the last. At the sixth in the terrace she stopped and turned to look at the door. She paused and looked a final time at the small white card. Looking up she spotted the neat bronze numbers perched just above the doorway. She stepped forward and pressed the doorbell to the right of the dark blue door. Inside the dwelling a double chime sounded. While she waited she shuffled her feet, not because she was trying to keep warm but because she was nervous.

Inside the building every movement of the woman as she had approached the house had been carefully observed. From an upper room the man had a perfect view of what was happening outside. It was not his usual practice to observe a client in such a way, but the phone call a little over an hour ago had left him intrigued. As it was clear that time would be of the very essence he had decided to begin his assessment even before his client had introduced herself.

Damien Palmer had finished business for the day some time before the phone had started ringing. Indeed he had been in the shower and had only just managed to intervene before the answer-phone would have taken the message. Now he was dressed for the evening. Smart casual wear had seemed to him to be the order of the day. As he watched the woman approach the house he detected the anxiety in her stride, and the one moment she glanced upwards he saw the strain in her face. There was perhaps, for a fleeting moment, something else, but Palmer could not be sure what.

The doorbell rang a second time and Palmer was already at the bottom of the stairs. He passed his office where the door was still ajar. The beginnings of the shelves of leather bound books could just be depicted. Had the door been completely open the full grandeur of his collection would have been evident. Not only that but the oak desk that grandly occupied the centre of the room added to the appearance of opulence. On the desk were two objects. The first looked like it belonged there. The ink blotter had been recently refreshed and was neatly lined up, a pristine sheet of blotting paper evident to the observer. The second object looked incongruous, for it belonged to a different era. The small black box lay closed on the right side of the desk. To Palmer this was possibly the most important piece of equipment he possessed. It was his lifeline to so much. Once activated, the lap top computer provided him with a lot of what was needed for him to do his job.

The door was not locked and even before the tones of the second chime had passed into history Palmer was looking out at his new client.

"Mr. Palmer?" she enquired purposefully.

"Damien Palmer at your service, and I take it that you are Miss Helen Cavendish?"

"You take it correctly. Thank you for seeing me at such short notice. Mr. Goodland spoke very highly of you. I hope you can help."

"Yes, well he would, wouldn't he? Oh, I am sorry, do come in."

"Thank you." The door closed behind the woman as she entered the hallway. "And why would he think highly of you, if you don't mind me asking?"

"Well," he paused for a moment, "it's nothing really."

"It may be nothing to you Mr. Palmer, but as my liberty may depend on your skills I think I have a right to know."

"Coffee? Tea perhaps? Please, do go in." Palmer gestured towards his office and even pushed the door open.

"Coffee, thank you."

"Fine. Please do take a seat, I won't be a minute."

"But you still haven't told me why my solicitor thinks so highly of you."

"I will do in the fullness of time. Not that we have much of it. First though, coffee."

He allowed her to enter the room and then made his exit to the kitchen. In fact he always had a percolator running and the coffee was already prepared, but this was one of his idiosyncrasies, allowing his client time to settle down. "After all," he had reasoned not half an hour earlier, "it might be the last decent cup of coffee she gets for a long while." He sat in the kitchen for a couple of minutes waiting. There was no real need to rush at this precise moment. The rush would come later. Mr. David Goodland had been quite sure of that. Palmer already had one advantage over the woman in his study. Goodland had phoned him while she was evidently in his company. His tone of voice had expressed the urgency of the matter and he had been very persuasive in getting Palmer to see his client that same evening. But the real advantage was the fact that with his client already on her way Goodland had taken the trouble to ring a second time to give Palmer more comprehensive details of the situation. In fact the conversation had taken several minutes and Palmer had only just begun to form a plan of action when the woman had arrived.

The coffee ruse was simply giving him a few moments to think.

"Coffee. I hope you like ground. I can't stand that awful instant stuff you get so much of these days."

"Ground coffee is just fine, thank you." Cavendish was sitting on the "interview" seat that faced the desk.

"White? Sugar?"

"White, no sugar, thanks you." Though evidently nervous, her voice was clear and polite.

The preliminaries over, Palmer sidled into his well-upholstered leather swivel chair and turned to face his client.

"Miss Cavendish I understand that you are in the gravest of situations and that you need my services to help you out of the gravity. Is that correct?"

"Yes Mr. Palmer, in a nutshell that is correct." She reached down to the bag that she had deposited on the floor. She pulled open the top and rummaged inside for a moment. She withdrew her hand that held in it an A4 sized manila envelope. She handed it across the desk. "Mr. Goodland asked me to give you this," she concluded.

"Oh good, now if you would give me just one moment to look at this," he began as he slit open the top of the sealed envelope, "and then you can tell me all about it from the very beginning."

He observed that the front of the letter had his name neatly typed in the middle, and curiously on the top had been hastily scrawled the two words "By Hand" in black ball-pen. He opened the envelope and carefully extracted the contents. The two pictures he scanned over and put to the back of the pile. He hastily read the introductory letter, though there was nothing in its content that he was not already aware of. He found the cheque that the letter promised. The thousand pounds would probably cover most of his immediate disbursements and in any event he knew that the budget for this case was significantly greater. He then focused on a report. It was not particularly long and having scanned it he looked up at his new client.

"And so Miss Cavendish, your version of events?" His enquiry carried with it a smile that was deliberately disarming but not overly friendly.

She took a couple of sips of coffee and began her story. As she spoke, Palmer made a few notes. He was a quick writer but not particularly neat. Her story continued for some fifteen minutes and as she told it she slowly, but perceptibly, became more agitated.

"And the long and the short of it is this," she said finally. "If you can't help me then I will go down for something I didn't do and the real criminal will get away with it. In short Mr. Palmer, I need an alibi, because it was sixteen months ago and I haven't got a clue where I was or what I was doing at the time of the accident."

"Hmm, and why the urgency tonight?"

"Well," she paused, "after the inquest it looked like the whole thing was a terrible accident. Now, though, in the past few weeks there's been that awful story put out," and she pointed at the report Palmer was once again holding. "It's anonymous of course but it suggests I arranged for them to be killed, and it's not true." By now the woman had started to sob, the faint streaks of tears falling down her cheeks. Anyway Mr. Goodland found out today that a writ has been issued for my arrest. Indeed, Mr. Goodland feels it would be best if I went and surrendered voluntarily, but, oh dear I don't know what to do."

"A tricky one I admit. And you do realise that by giving you this chance to speak to me your solicitor has placed himself in a very awkward position?"

"He has?" The woman looked puzzled.

"Of course." Palmer sounded surprised at the woman's apparent ignorance. "He knows about the writ and has had contact with you. He has a duty to contact the police. In fact, he could well have placed himself in a very difficult situation."

"But my visit to him was strictly off the record. There is no record of it, or of my coming here."

"That's as may be, but there is always a risk. Someone could have been outside his offices."

"But I didn't meet him there."

"No. Really?" The question was made with a mixture of surprise at the revelation and also a degree of incredulity. "Forgive me but this letter of introduction has been typed, and so has the envelope. Also your solicitor phoned me from his offices, I checked just to be sure."

"Oh that was easy. We actually met somewhere completely away from his offices, just because he was sure they are being watched. He had the letter and envelope prepared for me before I met him and all he did was set the Call Forward facility of his office phone to call you, and then he phoned his

11

office from his mobile phone. I'd have thought you'd have known about those kinds of things." Her voice was almost triumphant, but the tinge of anxiety remained and she continued to sob at intervals.

"That is very clever indeed. Perhaps your solicitor has missed his vocation. For your sake, I hope he hasn't. But why all the secrecy?"

"For the simple reason I had to talk to you before I got arrested. The rest of my life depended on it. You've got to find me that alibi."

"I see." Palmer rubbed the back of his neck as he contemplated the situation. "Now we must consider the idea of turning yourself in. On the one hand your solicitor is right, but on the other it's going to make talking to you a lot trickier. Is there anything you haven't told me that I should know about?"

"I don't think so."

"And you say your flat was searched thoroughly by the police straight after the accident and they found nothing?"

"That's correct."

"That was sixteen months ago, so they are sure to want to search it again. I need three hours. Can you give me that?"

"I suppose so."

"There must be no supposing about it. Those three hours are vital. Can you give me three hours, or not?

"Yes. I'll just go to ground for a bit."

"Excellent. In that case, can I borrow your flat keys for a minute?" Even as he was asking Palmer was opening a drawer on the left side of his desk.

"Now, you're not supposed to see what happens next." With that he took the two keys that she proffered and lifted the lid of the first of the two little metal boxes he had extracted. With infinite care he gently pressed the first key into the waxy substance in the box. That done he did the same with the second. When both impressions had been made he took a tissue and some spirit and carefully cleaned both keys before handing them back to the owner.

"Now, Miss Cavendish, do I have your permission to enter your premises?"

"Of course. What should I do next?"

"Well, I would suggest that you find somewhere to rest for a few hours, a pub or cafe, and then go home to bed. In the morning you should go back to Mr. Goodland and ask him to accompany you to the police station. I promise you, when you get home you will not know I've been there."

With that Palmer rose from the desk. The two boxes lay where he had left them. He ushered the woman to the door and bade her farewell. As he shut the door the genial smile on his face faded as he prepared for the task ahead. He knew he had to work fast and that in all probability he was too late anyway. He also knew that he had been less than honest with the woman and that it was very likely she would never know whether he had been to the flat or not, but he had not the heart to tell her what was likely to happen that evening.

Palmer worked quickly. In a few minutes he had poured a small quantity of molten metal into the moulds he had made. The metal spat at him as he poured it in. Then he waited for ten interminable minutes while the metal cooled. While it cooled he busied himself around his residence. Quickly he assembled the equipment he would need. He checked the camera was loaded, and that the flashlight and tape-machine were in working order. For some reason he also always carried a notebook, though he rarely wrote in it. The entire collection was soon stowed in a nondescript, brown, top-opening brief case. Then, and with great care, he lifted the new keys out of the moulds. He looked at them with the scrutiny of an expert. Satisfied, he placed both keys in his pocket and in a moment had left his terraced house.

He walked quickly but none too hurriedly to the nearest tube station. He had a good memory and knew exactly where he was heading. He carried the address in his wallet but was sure he would not need to check its details. As he walked he kept watching; watching in case he was being watched. After all, the writ must have been issued some three or four hours earlier and in any event from the documents he had seen that evening it seemed more than likely that someone other than the police were more than a little bit interested in his new client. Palmer considered that it was quite possible that the woman had been followed to his house. If so, then he could be followed now. By the time he reached the station he was virtually sure that he had walked unobserved.

The tube journey was short, a mere five stops, and Palmer alighted. With him came a few commuters finding their way home. It was a cool evening and no one seemed in the mood for conversation, not that commuters seemed to converse much anyway. As if this was the same journey that he had made every day for a few years, Palmer strode up the stairs out of the station. At the entrance was a concourse that led out into the taxi parking area. Beyond the taxi ranks was the High Street. Palmer walked out of the station and passed the taxis. Once on the road he turned right as if walking up into Wimbledon Village. Crossing a set of traffic lights and then a second set he walked quickly as the red bus came into view. He had just reached the bus stop when the bus pulled up.

"A stroke of luck", he whispered to himself. "Could have waited ages here at this time of night". He entered the bus through the front door and stated his destination before paying the fare. Looking round he eventually took a seat at the rear of the compartment and sat back to observe his fellow passengers. His observations were not totally benign. It was not just that he had a genuine curiosity about other people, but on more than one occasion his life had been saved because he had spotted something in time. Now he looked around, casually but with purpose. The bus began its climb up the hill into the village.

He watched carefully as the bus passed through the village, the narrow street with the mini roundabouts at either end, past the familiar pub and stables on the left, and then on towards the common. The bus stopped briefly at the allotted places but with so few passengers each stop was more of a formality than a necessity. Finally Palmer stood up and pressed the red button signalling the driver he wished to alight at the next stop. He watched purposefully as the bus slowed down. He knew where the flat was located. It was normally a short walk of no more than five minutes from the bus stop but he wanted to be sure he was not being followed. So, instead of taking the short, direct, route, Palmer decided a more circuitous approach would be preferable. The bus had stopped now and the doors hissed open. He stepped down onto the pavement and stood there as the bus continued on its journey. With the road clear he crossed over and began the route to the flat. Although time was short he wanted to be sure he was on his own, though once the bus had started up again it seemed evident that he was. He walked purposefully down the road, taking first a left turn and then a right turn, until he found himself in the road he was searching for. He passed a grey Volvo. As he did so he noticed that the driver was reading a street map.

Somewhere in Palmer's brain an alarm bell started to ring. He was now less than two minutes walk from the flat and he knew the street map gag of old. It was one he had performed countless times, and seeing it performed here in the street as he passed by sent his adrenaline racing to a new level. As a direct consequence his walk became even brisker. He was fully fifty yards past the grey Volvo when he heard an engine start behind him. Not looking round, yet listening with great intent, he continued to walk. He saw the block of flats across the road from where he was walking, but decided to ignore them for now. The engine was still sounding behind him; a low, slow sound. When he was a few yards past the block of flats the car suddenly roared its engine and passed by him. He breathed a little easier as the car disappeared from view.

Turning back on his tracks he made straight for the flats. He passed through the gap in the low hedge at the front and stood at the front door.

"Damn", he cursed softly to himself. "Might have known there'd be one of those, and I didn't even think to ask her for the number." The entry-phone and combination number pad waited silently. He looked at the buttons and then around him. He spotted the bundle of newspapers lying to the side of the door and picked them up. Although the little white name plate next to Cavendish's flat number was not filled in it did not bother him. Most of them were blank, as if the owners were trying to retain some kind of anonymity whilst in their dwellings. He pressed the top buzzer, more out of habit than anything.

"Hello." The female voice crackled slightly over the intercom.

"Paperboy," Palmer introduced himself. "Guardian. Can you let me in to drop them off."

"Don't you normally leave them outside?" The voice sounded annoyed at having been interrupted by a mere paperboy.

"Yeah, have done up 'til now. But the boss says we have to put 'em inside if we can, "cause when it rains they get wet otherwise." Over the intercom his voice sounded just like a teenage boy to the occupant of the penthouse flat.

"Oh well, in that case I suppose I'd better open it for you."

"Thanks." Even as he spoke he heard the buzzer indicate that the magnetic lock had been released for a few seconds. He pushed on the door and entered the block of flats. Once inside he held the door for a few seconds and then let it shut behind him.

The flats were arranged on four floors. There were four flats on each of the first three floors, with a single penthouse suite on the top floor, filling the eaves of the five years old building. Cavendish lived at flat 7, which, Palmer had reckoned, was on the first floor. For a moment as he started to climb the stairs he wondered how well the occupants knew each other. Quite well, he guessed, as he reached the first landing. He pushed open the fire door and entered the common landing for flats five to eight. The flats were arranged two on each side, with a window at the opposite end of the landing to the fire door. He walked towards the window and glanced out. It looked quiet outside, probably because at that precise moment it was.

His gloved hand rummaged in his pockets and sought out the two keys he had fabricated a little over an hour earlier. Holding the keys he glanced at his watch briefly before inserting the "Chubb" type key in the lower lock. Gently he started to turn it. The key moved a fraction and then stuck. He tried turning it in the other direction but was greeted with the same result. He removed the key from the lock and held it up to the landing light for closer inspection.

The key had a small fragment of moulding covering one of the gaps between the key's teeth. Palmer reached into his pocket and extracted the small file that he had learned to carry for such events. He gently filed the fragment of metal and after a minute re-inspected the key under the light. Satisfied with his work he again tried the key in the lock. This time it turned easily and he heard the lock slide open. He withdrew the key and was about to turn his attention to the upper "Yale" type lock when he heard the outer door open below him. Breathing somewhat more quickly he placed the second of his keys in the lock. With a quick and silent prayer that this one would work he started to turn it. He could hear footsteps on the stairway below. The key began to turn but the lock seemed unduly stiff. Whilst Palmer did not want to turn the key too aggressively, as he was aware that his home made varieties were not that strong, the urgency of the situation demanded speed rather than expediency.

"Here goes nothing," he muttered as he exerted more pressure on the key. The steps were now getting closer. The door gave as the latch yielded under the turning key. Palmer passed inside without a pause and gently closed the door. From within he placed the first key into the lower lock and in a moment the door was securely locked. Palmer heard the fire door on the landing opening and then heard one of the other flats being entered. Finally he dared to breathe. Still wearing the light gloves he pulled the small flashlight torch from the right pocket of his coat. Switching it on he quickly picked out the details of the hallway of the flat. It was just as his client had described it.

He felt in his pocket and turned on the tape recorder. He pulled the slim tie-clip microphone out of the pocket and fastened it to his lapel.

In a matter of a few moments Palmer had entered the woman's bedroom. His examination was as swift as it was thorough and all the time he muttered his observations into the microphone. In less than two minutes he had checked the drawers and wardrobe. His gloved hand felt between the bed base and the mattress but found nothing. The carpet was stuck to the concrete floor and so could not be used for hiding things under. In seconds he had entered the bathroom. Again his examination lasted a couple of minutes and again he exited the room having found nothing of interest. There were now two rooms left and a small storage cupboard. The cupboard was neatly arranged. Sheets, blankets and towels were neatly stacked on the upper shelf. Below the shelves was a vacuum cleaner, an ironing board and a couple of large, blue vases. Again Palmer made a quick examination but found nothing. He glanced at his watch by the torchlight but appeared unconcerned. With luck, he thought, he had another hour and a half before he might be disturbed – with luck.

The kitchen was clean and tidy. The cupboards contained exactly what would be expected in a kitchen, and nothing else. Palmer methodically examined each and every drawer and still he continued to talk into the microphone. Finally he had completed his search of the kitchen and still had not found what he was looking for.

He entered the final room of the flat a little more than ten minutes after he had entered the flat. The lounge/diner was again clean and tidy. The furniture comprised a two-seater sofa, a casual chair, a dining table and four chairs, a bookcase, TV and Video ensemble and a midi hi-fi unit. Palmer observed all this and then turned his attentions to the bookcase. There was only one shelf of books, the other shelves containing glassware and other assorted ornaments. Palmer duly began to methodically examine each book in turn. Removing the book he turned it upside down and then shook it. The first half dozen books yielded nothing. The seventh book was a slim paperback and as Palmer performed his ritual act of shaking the book a small piece of paper fell to the floor. Palmer picked it up, smiled slightly and carefully placed it on the table. His small pocket camera was soon retrieved from the brown case and in a moment he had recorded the contents of the piece of paper. This action complete, he returned the piece of paper to the book and returned the book to the shelf. He continued with the search and found three further pieces of paper that interested him. He meticulously photographed each item as he uncovered it. All the time the tape recorder was noting down his audible observations.

Finally Palmer turned his attention to the sofa. He removed the cushions and felt carefully down the side. On the second side he examined he withdrew his hand holding a small dark-blue pocket diary. Looking at it he let out a soft whistle. He thumbed through the pages. It was indeed a diary. A diary for the previous year, and as he looked at it he noted that his client was one of those people who kept notes for virtually every day. He reached the back of the book and found the address pages. On them were neatly scribed the names of more than thirty people. Palmer looked at it as he spoke.

"This diary," he continued to speak into the microphone, "contains far more information than I can copy at this time. It will have to be removed from the scene for more detailed examination and then dealt with at a later date. I simply don't have the time to record all its details at this time."

Palmer then placed the notebook in a clear plastic envelope that he then folded and placed carefully in his inside pocket.

He turned to leave the lounge and as he did so he heard the buzzer on the outer door as its sound broke the silence of the evening. He waited quietly in the dark for two minutes until he could be sure that whoever was entering the building had also entered their flat. He reached the front door of the flat and out of habit peered through the spy-hole. Standing outside the door were two tall gentlemen dressed in the uniform of the Metropolitan Police. Palmer stopped breathing and very quietly retreated back to the lounge.

He waited for perhaps five seconds before he heard the first knock on the door. As it sounded his heart began to beat faster. He could do nothing but wait and hope that they would not try to gain access to the flat. If they did, he reasoned, he could face a few difficult questions about his presence there, and his possession of the diary. He waited quietly, listening for any sound. The lounge door was open and he heard the second knock, a shade harder than the first but still polite.

"Can't see if there's any lights on inside." Palmer could just see the landing light as one of the gentlemen outside pushed open the letterbox to look inside. "Doesn't look like it, I can't see a thing, and it's so dark."

"Hmm. Let me have a look."

The letterbox was closed momentarily as the two gentlemen outside swapped positions.

"Nah, you're right. She can't be in. Better radio it in. Oscar two zero to Charlie Foxtrot Lima, over."

Palmer could almost hear the crackling, muffled noise of a response.

"There's no response from the flat Serge. Appears to be in darkness and there's no sounds within. What now, over?"

Again the muffled crackling response was virtually inaudible from within the flat.

"Oscar two zero, understood."

"Well?"

"We have to wait outside for a bit. They're still trying to locate her brief but he isn't at home either. So we wait. Let's go."

Palmer heard the fire door on the landing being opened and then closed, and a few seconds later he heard the buzzer as the outside door was opened. He stood up and carefully went to look out of the darkened window. He saw the two police officers return to their car that was situated just to the left of the flats.

"Right," he said to himself, "time to go." With that Palmer quickly returned to the front door, peered through the spy-hole and in less than thirty seconds had passed through the door and re-locked it. He pocketed the two keys and began to descend the stairs. His brown case swung loosely at his side, and he looked exactly as if he were an insurance salesman leaving a client.

He reached the front door of the block of flats and pressed the door release button. The sound of the buzzer became muted as the door closed behind him. He walked briskly, but not too quickly, past the police car. He noticed that the car still contained two occupants. He remained unchallenged as he walked back to the bus stop. There was something he had to do, and he had to do it soon, but he could not do it where he was. His task would have to wait until the end of the bus ride. The urgency of the matter was still occupying Palmer's mind as the red bus pulled up at the stop. Palmer ascended the step and paid the fare back to the station. As he did so a second bus drew up though this was travelling in the opposite direction. Palmer noted the young woman standing on the second bus and went to sit at the back of his own bus. He looked out of the back window, distracted for a moment.

"Damn," he muttered to himself as he recognised the woman. "Less time than I had hoped. What the hell is she doing back here so early?" His voice was hushed and totally inaudible to the person sitting at the front of the seating area. "She could have given me another hour."

The bus began its journey to the station. Palmer became aware of a dark coloured car that seemed to be following the bus. He glanced out of the window but could not obtain a clear view of the car's driver. Also the car was travelling at a sufficient distance to make the index number hard to decipher. Palmer discretely maintained his observation as the bus passed through the village and then descended the hill towards the station. At each stop along the way the car overtook, but regained its position after the next side road. Palmer removed his gloves as the bus neared his stop and then retrieved his return ticket for the train. There was little point in running, he had decided, as the frequency of trains at that time of evening meant if he was being followed that his pursuer would have ample time to purchase a ticket and follow him. He formulated a strategy as the bus slowed to a halt. As before on the journey, the car passed the bus and Palmer noticed there were two occupants. They looked young and were casually dressed.

Palmer descended from the bus. The dark car was now some fifty yards ahead of the bus and travelling slowly. Palmer observed that the passenger was looking back at the bus. As Palmer stepped off the bus onto the pavement he saw the passenger door start to open. The bus stop was no more than fifty yards from the entrance to the station and Palmer covered the distance in less than ten seconds. As he ran he imagined the car's passenger following him. He entered the station and quickly passed the ticket barrier. He surmised that if he was being followed then there was a realistic chance that whoever was following him would know where he lived. He looked quickly at the information monitors and simultaneously heard the voice announcing the imminent departure of a train. He ran for all he was worth onto the platform and just made it to the last carriage as the automatic doors were closing. Breathing heavily he sat down on an empty row of seats. After a moment he looked around and realised he was quite alone in the carriage.

"Thank God" he panted. He reached into the inner pocket of his coat and withdrew his mobile phone. "And thank God for you too," he muttered as he hastily dialled a number. After a moment he made contact.

"Goodland?" His voice was still affected by his breathless state, and though his question was terse it was nonetheless as polite as he could manage.

"Yes," came the equally short reply.

"Where are you, this is Palmer."

"I know."

"Can you talk?"

"Not really, it's a bit chilly up here and I can't hear you very well."

"Are you alone?"

"Not exactly, can I ring you back?"

"Yes. Before you go, mission accomplished."

"Sorry." Palmer could not be sure if the voice was apologetic or questioning his last utterance.

"I said mission accomplished. I'll talk to you tomorrow."

This time there was no response and the line went dead. Palmer replaced the phone in his inner pocket and sat back to contemplate the evening's events.

The train passed through several stations. Palmer decided that he would deliberately not alight at his own stop just in case someone was waiting for him, which seemed likely following the events in Wimbledon. The train continued its journey towards the very heart of London. Palmer knew precisely where he was going and had already decided what he had to do next. The brown bag stood on the train's floor neatly sandwiched between Palmer's legs. As the journey progressed he began to relax.

Finally, after about forty-five minutes, the train pulled into Victoria station. Palmer alighted and made his way to the Northbound Victoria line platform. The "blue line" train turned up a few minutes later and Palmer continued his journey. He could be certain now that he was not being followed. At Green Park Palmer alighted and made his way to the surface. He walked briskly to a block of flats and pressed the doorbell of the flat he wanted. He waited. After a minute he pressed the bell button a second time. After a few seconds there was a crackling sound on the intercom.

"Uh-huh." The voice from inside was barely audible.

"Jane, its Damien, can I come in?"

"Uh-huh." The voice sounded weary and disinterested but in a moment the lock on the front door to the block of flats was released and as Palmer slipped inside the sound of the buzzer faded into the night.

Although a fairly modern block of flats the inside of the woman's flat was sparsely furnished, functional rather than homely. The door was open, waiting for him, by the time he had climbed the two flights of stairs. He pushed the door wide, and closed it firmly behind him. Once inside he took off his coat and went into the lounge.

"Trouble?" The woman's voice came from the kitchen area to the side of the lounge and dining room.

"Sort of, but it's nothing for you to worry about." Palmer lied, but he didn't want to worry the woman.

"Yeah, sure it isn't. Coffee, or something stronger?"

"Something stronger if you have it, and coffee would be nice too."

"Good old Damien, never change, do you?"

The woman appeared in the archway that separated the kitchenette from the lounge. Dressed in a night shirt and hastily adorned bathrobe, her dishevelled long brown hair gave Palmer the clear impression that she had retired for the night some time before his arrival.

"Sorry, Jane, did I get you up?" His question was meant to be rhetorical, but it still received a response.

"Not really, I was just reading. Nothing on worth watching so I got ready for bed early. Hang on a tick." With that she disappeared into the kitchenette. The disembodied voice continued, "You know where the booze is. Help yourself, and I'll have a whisky while you're at it."

"Okay. Anything in it?"

"You should know the answer to that by now." She reappeared in the archway holding two mugs of steaming coffee. "I take it neat, just like my men." She smiled wickedly.

Palmer missed her smile as at that moment his back was turned away from the kitchenette while he concentrated on pouring the Whisky into the half size straight tumblers.

"Now, tell me what the trouble is." The woman had sat on the sofa and beckoned to the detective to join her.

"Not much really, I was just doing a job for someone tonight and things got a bit out of hand.

Actually I was followed by a couple of unsavoury blokes and had to use the trains to get away. Now, cheers." With that he raised his glass and took a mouthful of the brown liquid.

"So, are you staying over?"

"Depends on you. I certainly can't go back home tonight. Just in case they know where I live."

"And you weren't followed here?"

"No chance."

"Sure?"

"Yes, I'm sure. It took me the best part of two hours to get here and I'm absolutely sure that no-one, and I mean no-one, was following me."

"Well, I hope you are right." The woman moved a shade closer to the man and gently placed a hand on his knee. " Okay, you can stay, if you're sure."

"I'm sure, and thanks."

"That's all right. It seems a long time, but then what are friends for." Her voice sounded hurt, but Palmer knew that this was just her way.

They sat and chatted for several minutes, as if passing the time of day. Having known each other for over seven years they had plenty to talk about. Finally the whisky had been drunk and the mugs were drained of the coffee.

"Right," the woman said," I'm for bed." She stood up and Palmer stood with her. She turned to look at him and instinctively took a half step towards him. She reached up on tiptoe and in a moment had given him the briefest of pecks on the cheek. "Night then," she continued as she feigned to pull away. As she did so he reached an arm around her back and pulled her close to him. He felt her firm, shapely body pressed against his and he looked into her face. He bent forwards slightly until his face was looking straight at hers and then he drew her even closer. Their lips met in a long and passionate kiss. Finally he released his hold on her.

"It's been a long time, Jane. Too long."

"Yeah. Too long." She reached forward and again their lips were joined in passion, though this time the contact was more frenetic. They were still holding each other as she led him to the bedroom.

"Just for tonight," she whispered as she kicked the bedroom door shut behind her. In less than two minutes the bedroom light was turned off, and with it the night descended.

***

Outside, the greyness of the evening had finally given way to light drizzle. The drizzle in turn had become steady rainfall and in the middle of it the breeze had strengthened, making it a cold, wet night for anyone out of doors. The light in the second floor flat was still visible from the road as the small dark car pulled into the metered parking space a few yards from the building's entrance. The car had two occupants and they sat there in the darkness, the music from the tape in the car's cassette player barely audible from outside the vehicle. The rain was falling now, and the spots of rain quickly obscured the view from the windscreen.

"It's eleven. How long do we give it?" The passenger looked slightly the younger of the two. As he spoke he lit a cigarette and the glow from the end could be seen some distance away as he inhaled.

"All night if needs be." His companion sat relaxed in the driver's seat. He too was smoking. In the feint light from the nearest street lamp an observer would just have seen the two inch scar on the left side of his neck. "The boss wants this guy watched, at any cost. Apparently he has stuff of interest on him."

"Oh, great. Another night parked up with you."

"You'll get paid for it."

"Too bloody right I will. I'll make sure of that."

"Yeah, well that's your problem. I never asked you to vault the gates and make an arse of yourself. You had time to get a ticket. You didn't have to go and jump the bleeding gates."

"All right, but I was just following him."

"Yeah, and you lost him."

"Weren't my fault. Got us here though."

"Yeah. Pure luck I'd say. And we don't even know he's in there."

"He is."

"How the hell can you be sure of that? He could be anywhere."

"He's in there. He was spotted at the station and we know she's a friend. Come on, at this time of night where else would he go?"

"Maybe."

"He's in there. You don't believe me? There's only one way to be sure about that. Go and kick the offing door in and find out."

"Hold on, don't be stupid. The boss said to wait, and wait we will."

The occupants of the small car were evidently a mismatched pair. An observer outside would have seen their gesticulations and mouthed conversation. Their animated behaviour indicated a good deal of friction between them. The rain continued to fall, heavier now than when they had first drawn into the kerb. The windscreen wipers were now in continuous use, the rhythmic sound of the motor unheard above the music from the cassette player. The occupants waited. As they waited they kept an eye on the second floor flat. At eleven thirty they noted that the light in the living room was turned off. From the front the flat was now shrouded in darkness.

"Okay Charlie, one of us has to go and check the back and as it's raining it can be you." The driver looked at his fellow occupant in the car and smiled wickedly.

"No chance, get wet yourself."

"You've simply got no respect. You've got two minutes or you're out." The driver reached into his jacket pocket and pulled out a mobile phone. "Is that clear?"

"Yeah. Bastard." With that the younger occupant opened the passenger door. He walked away from the car without bothering to close the door. The rain was now falling heavily and the chill wind made the rain feel biting cold.

"Shut the offing door." The driver could have saved his breath, as there was no way his colleague could have heard him above the taped music. He reached over and pulled the door closed.

The younger man half ran the twenty or so yards past the flat. As he did so he came to a narrow passage that led to a walled garden behind the buildings. He turned sharply into the alley and ran to its farther end. Turning, he looked back up at the flats just in time to see the light in the back room of the second floor flat being extinguished. As the rain battered against his body he shuddered before running back up the alley to the relative warmth of the car.

"Just turned out the back room light. Gone to bed I'd say."

"Or getting ready to run. We wait five minutes then I'll phone the boss."

The five minutes passed slowly and without event. Finally the driver pressed the redial button on the mobile phone and a minute later started to speak.

"George here, we're outside the chicks flat in Green Park". Don't know for sure if he's in there, but we think he is. Harry spotted him at the tube walking this way. Lights have been out for a couple of minutes now and there's nothing happening. What do you want us to do?"

The passenger waited anxiously, unable to hear the reply.

"Yeah, okay then. Talk to you tomorrow then." He pressed a button and returned the phone to his jacket. "Boss says we can bugger off, but he wants us back in the morning to talk with the chick."

"Yeah." The sound of the car starting up went unheard in the second floor flat. The occupants were otherwise pre-occupied at that precise moment, seven years of friendship and a mutual lust for passion making both of them oblivious to anything that was happening beyond the room they occupied.

Chapter 2

The early morning rays of light filtered weakly into the flat. The woman was the first to awaken, turning in the bed and gently caressing the man. He too stirred and turned to cuddle the woman.

"I've got work to get to," she said pushing him gently away.

"Go on, just ten minutes won't hurt."

"Yeah it will, and any way, you've got some things to do as well haven't you."

"Yeah, suppose so."

Half an hour later Palmer left the flat. He turned out onto the road and passed the small dark car. Its presence went unnoticed, as he was preoccupied with his thoughts. Also he failed to notice the two occupants sitting in the front seat. Palmer turned the corner and walked onwards to the station. As he did so the driver and passenger of the car stepped out onto the road and pavement respectively.

Palmer continued his walk to the station. He greeted the newspaper salesman at the station's entrance and purchased one of the more up-market tabloids. He barely noticed the benign smile that was on the face of the seller as he took his change. The journey back to his own home was uneventful, though Palmer kept a close eye on all his travelling companions, and did his best to make sure that he was not followed.

Once inside he threw his coat on the chair and dialled the number of Goodland, Peasbody and

Nash, Solicitors. The woman's voice on the other end of the line was civil.

"Goodland, Peasbody, and Nash. How may I help you?"

"David Goodland please," Damien replied in an equally civilised though more hurried manner.

"And who's calling?"

"Damien Palmer."

"Thank-you Mr. Palmer, one moment please." The secretary's unhurried manner was beginning to annoy Palmer, who's own manner indicated a significant degree of urgency. The line went dead for a few moments.

"Hello, Mr. Palmer."

"Yes"

"I'm sorry but Mr. Goodland hasn't arrived yet. Would you like to leave a message?"

"No thanks."

"Would you like him to call you when he does get in."

"No, it's all right. I'll try ringing back later."

"Very well, and thank you for calling." The line went dead and Palmer replaced the receiver on its cradle.

The call over, Palmer went over to his coat and extracted the camera from the outer pocket. He took the stairs to the upper floor two at a time. The smallest of the three bedrooms had been converted into a primitive dark room and Palmer set about developing the film of the previous evening's activities.

A little more than half an hour later the film had been developed and Palmer was scrutinising the negatives. He rarely printed these as it was not usually necessary.   More often than not the negatives gave him the details he required. Palmer returned to his ground floor office and made the second phone call of the day.

"Good morning, this is Goodland, Peasbody and Nash. How may I help you?"

"David Goodland please," Damien replied, noting that the female voice was the same as the one he had spoken to earlier.

"And who's calling?"

"Damien Palmer."

"Thank-you Mr. Palmer, one moment please." This time the voice sounded somewhat ruffled.

"Hello." The voice was male but unrecognised to Palmer. "John Nash, can I help you Mr. Palmer?"

"I was trying to contact David Goodland. I'm an acquaintance."

"I'm sorry. Mr. Goodland isn't in the office today."

"Oh. You don't know where he is, do you? It's quite important."

"I'm sorry, but I don't. He's not listed for court or holiday. He may be at home. You have his number?"

"Yes, thanks. If he does show up could you ask him to ring me please."

"Yes. Mr. Palmer, wasn't it? I'll leave a note with his secretary."

"Thank you and goodbye." Palmer replaced the receiver only to pick it up again a second later. He listened briefly for the dial tone and then dialled a fresh number. After a few seconds the phone started to ring. Palmer let it ring for almost a minute but received no answer. Finally he replaced the receiver. He reclined in his chair, clasped his hands and pressed the two index fingers against his pursed lips as he began to contemplate the situation.

***

As Palmer had left the flat earlier that morning the occupants of the small dark car had watched him go. They watched as he turned the corner and then they had waited. They waited for just over five minutes before they made their way nonchalantly to the same entrance that Palmer had left. The larger of the occupants pushed the door. It held fast, the magnetic lock preventing entry. The postman was making his way slowly down the road as the younger man pressed the buzzer for flat five. In a few moments the sound of the male occupant could be heard.

"Yes," he enquired.

"Postman. I'm the relief so I don't know the number. Can you let me in?"

"Okay. Hang on a second."

A moment later the buzzer sounded on the door as the magnetic lock was released. The two men passed inside and let the door swing closed.

"Easy" said the first man.

"Yeah. Now which flat?"

"Second floor left hand side."

The men climbed the stairs quickly. They had just reached the second floor and passed through the fire door when they heard the door to the left flat being opened.

The door was partly opened when the larger man pushed it with the full weight of his body. The

37

woman inside was immediately thrown off balance and fell backwards, stunned, shocked and bewildered all at the same time. As the door banged its way open under the force applied to it she fell back into the wall and was instantly winded.

It took maybe ten seconds for her to react. It was ten seconds too long, for in that time the two men had swiftly entered the flat and slammed the door shut behind them.

The woman looked at her assailants with sheer terror in her eyes. She made as if to cry out but the larger of the two men shoved her back against the wall and clasped his hand tightly over her mouth so that far from screaming she could barely breathe.

"Now listen to me," he whispered fiercely. "I'm gonna take this hand away and if you make a single noise then I'll break your neck. Understand?"

"Hmm," she struggled to mutter through the thickness of his hand. As she did so she tried to nod her head.

Slowly the hand was removed. By this time the smaller of the two men had already gone into the living room. As he did so he turned on the main light and swiftly pulled the curtains closed. He pulled a dining chair into the centre of the room just as the larger man escorted the woman into the room. He pushed her towards the chair and she fell into it. Roughly the younger man grabbed her hands and with some strong black tape tied them together behind the chair.

Somehow the woman started to recover from the shock. Her back ached from being pushed against the wall and she could taste blood, probably from the cut on her forehead she had received when the door had been roughly pushed open. Strangely she wasn't crying, possibly because she was too shocked. She looked up at her assailants. She did not recognise either of them, but in her dazed state she desperately tried to remember something she could use later to describe them.

"Now," said the larger man, "we want to have a little chat. You had someone stay here last night, didn't you."

"Maybe. What's it to do with you?" She gasped in pain as her hair was pulled from behind forcing her head backwards until she was staring at the ceiling.

"Just answer the questions. I don't have much time and we can get a lot rougher if we have to."

"Yes, I had someone stay here. So what?"

"And what was his name?"

"None of your business." The woman's resistance was impressive, but it earned her another eyeful of the ceiling as she again gasped in pain.

"Once more – his name."

"None of your business."

The smaller man still held her head back as the larger man walked round to her front. He took one side of her blouse in each hand and with one short definitive movement had ripped it apart, the buttons falling uselessly onto the floor.

"Once more – his name."

"Charles."

"Better. Charles who?"

"Charles. Just Charles. I picked him up yesterday. That's all I know."

"That's not all you know." The interrogators voice was becoming more and more agitated. As he

39

spoke his hands grasped her bra-covered breasts. "You've got a nice body and it's be a shame to re-arrange it. But we have our orders. His name?"

"Charles. He didn't give me another name."

"Liar", he hissed savagely. His grasp of her breasts was increased and he began to try to lift her off the chair. Her body rose as he pulled her upwards, her hands still tied behind her back. Finally, with tears of pain streaming down her face, she was standing.

"One last chance."

"I only know him as Charles. For God's sake I only met him yesterday."

The flat of the man's hand caught her across her face, splitting her lower lip. Under the weight of the slap she reeled round, dragging the chair with her. As she reeled the second slap forced her backwards again. Slowly a bruise started to form under her left eye.

"Finish her off." The taller man looked at the smaller one and walked out of the room. As he did so the smaller man dragged her to the table and forced her against it bending her over until her face was pushed into the wooden surface. He stood menacingly behind her and forced her legs apart.

When he'd finished with her he pulled her up and pushed her onto the settee. Without a word he found a tea towel from the kitchen and stuffed it unceremoniously into her mouth. Then he left the room and after a brief visit to the bathroom he found his companion.

"Find anything?"

"Nothing. You finish in there?"

"Nearly. Ready to go?"

"Yeah. No evidence?"

"Nah. And she isn't a hooker."

"Oh well, it don't matter. She isn't talking and there's nothing here."

"Yeah, guess so. Time to go."

"Yeah, let's do it."

The taller man pulled a small revolver from his coat pocket.

"You want me to do it for you?"

"Nah. Give it here." The smaller man reached out and took the revolver. He partly opened the lounge door until he could see the woman lying, crying, on the settee. He squeezed the trigger. The faint smell of smoke came from the barrel as he closed the door again.

The two assailants quickly left the flat. In the same way as they had arrived, so they left. The left the flat unseen and, despite the events of the previous twenty minutes, they went unheard.

***

Palmer sat motionless for nearly an hour. His eyes were closed in thought as if he were seeking some ethereal inspiration. Finally his eyes opened and he looked out of the window. The rain had started falling again. He looked at the negatives on the desk, picked them up and went back upstairs. He spent the next hour in the darkroom before he emerged holding a collection of enlarged prints. He took these back to the office and extracted the cassette recorder from the coat. He rewound the tape to the beginning and with the assembly of prints lying on his desk began to play back the monologue. It worried him that this case had started out as a simple request to provide a client of someone he knew professionally with an alibi for a tragic event sixteen months earlier. As it stood now it looked like something altogether more sinister, and for the life of him Palmer couldn't work out why – not yet.

As he listened intently to his own voice on the tape he observed the pictures that he had taken. It took maybe an hour and at the end of it he was still perplexed. During that hour he had also reread the case notes provided by his client's solicitor. As the tape came to an end, Palmer recalled his last conversation with Goodland the previous evening. Something about it being a "bit chilly up here, and I can't hear you very well."

It was now almost exactly three o'clock and Palmer knew he should be further advanced than he was in the case. He began to pace the room. He held the little diary that he had picked up the previous evening and he flicked through the pages of the address section. It was a long list, neatly hand written.

He walked the room's length maybe seven times before sitting down. Something, somewhere didn't fit in. There were just too many loose ends. He looked again at the notes the solicitor had given to Cavendish the night before. Cavendish! Suddenly it hit him. In the activity of the previous evening he had quite forgotten the obvious, and yet it was staring at him from the pages of the woman's previous year's diary. Why would anyone put their own name in the address section of their own diary? There it was, neatly printed – Helen Cavendish.

In a moment he had the phone propped up under his chin as he punched in a number. The phone rang but there was no reply. He tried another number with the same result.

"Damn. She must have been arrested, and with a solicitor that can't be found I can't get to her."

Palmer was just contemplating the situation when the phone rang. The man's voice was calm, relaxed even, and almost amiable, but the content of his speech was quite the opposite.

"Mr. Palmer?" He questioned.

"Yes." Palmer faltered as the unfamiliar voice continued.

"Mr. Damien Palmer, who last night stayed in a flat near Green Park?"

"Yes." Palmer was now sitting bolt upright with the microphone on the tape recorder pressed close to the mouthpiece.

"You may be interested to know that the woman who lives in that flat has had an accident. The same accident will also happen to anybody else you talk to regarding the Cavendish case. Do you understand?"

"Yes."

"Good. And you would be wise to stay away from the police as well."

"So, what do you want?"

With that the line went dead.

"Hello". The line was still dead.

Palmer relaxed for a moment. He swivelled round in the chair and pulled the curtains closed. Once sure that he could not be observed from outside the building, he dialled the number of the flat he had stayed the night at. There was no reply.

Palmer reached out and opened the laptop computer that had been sitting benignly on the desk the whole day. He waited patiently as the machine came to life. He pressed some buttons and the E-mail screen appeared. Quickly he typed in the address of the recipient and then typed out a short, innocuous looking message. Finally he pressed the "send" button and watched as the machine transmitted the message.

At least he now knew that there was something sinister about the mysterious Helen Cavendish even though he knew little else about the case. Suddenly a thought came to him. He rummaged around in his desk and brought out what looked like a CD. But this was no ordinary CD. Instead of music the disc was crammed full with information, the kind of information that Private Investigators love to handle. He pushed a button on the side of the computer and placed the CD on the tray that had appeared from the machine's innards. Then he gently pushed the edge of the tray so that it began to close. In a moment the screen filled with a new image and seconds later Palmer was able to type in the name of his client. He noted that the address that was retrieved was the same as the flat he had visited the previous evening. He also noted that a person with the same name and initials was listed at a further address some ten to fifteen miles away. He noted down the details provided. Using the machine's built in mouse he scanned across to a small image on the left of the screen. He double clicked the mouse on the icon and watched as another window opened up in front of him. This time he waited as the machine rapidly dialled a number and connected with another machine somewhere across London. As it did so the contents of the screen changed. Palmer again typed in his client's full name and waited for the machine to complete its search. It took perhaps thirty seconds before the screen was once again filled with information. This time it was a listing of a partnership.

He whistled softly to himself as he recognised the name of the other partner – Sharon Mortimer. As he scanned the screen he made notes on the sheet of paper to the side of the computer. The information logged, he then pressed more buttons, typed a different name, and again noted the results of the enquiry. After two further enquiries he finally ended the call and switched the computer off.

He looked at the sheet of paper with growing incredulity. He reached out for his brown brief case and pulled out the bundle of papers that related to his client.

He scanned these for perhaps the tenth time since he had received them. Then he looked at the two photographs. The first was of a woman. He referred to the letter that accompanied the picture and ten looked again at the woman's image. There was a striking resemblance to his client that was not lost on Palmer. The second picture was that of a man. He was in his mid-thirties, of average height and build. His light brown hair was neatly trimmed in a short style and in the picture he was casually, though smartly, dressed. Palmer took a good look at the two pictures. Although the report stated quite categorically that both people in the pictures had died on June 13th the previous year in a road accident, there was something about the pictures that made Palmer spend time in their scrutiny. Finally he put the pictures down and again picked up the report. There was not much detail. The report indicated that the male, one John Arthur Baker was found dead in the driver's seat of a blue BMW. The female, Samantha Elaine Baker, spouse of the male deceased, was found dead in the passenger seat of the same car. The car had apparently failed to negotiate a tight bend on a certain road, the name of which was not important. It had happened on the evening of June 13th sixteen months ago.

In all probability it was the result of a flash rainstorm about an hour before the time of the incident. The pathology report had failed to turn up anything untoward and the forensic analysis of the car indicated at the time of the first impact the car had been travelling in excess of 60 miles per hour, a speed that might have been considered somewhat high in view of the road conditions. The Coroner's report had concluded death was due to misadventure.

Palmer then looked at the information provided by Goodland. The charge against Helen Cavendish had arisen out of an incident a few days after the accident. It transpired that a credit card in the name of Samantha Baker had been used to try to obtain a significant purchase at Harrods. An alert shop assistant had made the usual checks and then called store detectives when the card check was returned without authorisation being given. The police had been called and Helen Cavendish had feigned ignorance. She had described the dinner party that had taken place the night before the fatal accident. She and Samantha had coincidentally taken the same handbag to the meal that was at a local restaurant. She presumed that they had picked up each other's bag by mistake. As she always had her keys in a coat or jacket pocket the mistake would have gone unnoticed by her until she needed money, the first time being the shopping visit. Still shocked by the news of the death she had not even noticed the switch then.

The various people concerned had been sympathetic to her statement and she had been released pending further investigation. After the inquest the matter of the credit card had been put aside as a seemingly genuine mistake.

The weeks had turned into sixteen months and then mysteriously and anonymously the police had received a letter stating that Cavendish had arranged for the murder of the Bakers. The letter was short and patchy but had warranted investigation. After a couple of weeks the police issued a warrant for her arrest in connection with the alleged murder of John and Samantha Baker.

That had been yesterday. The problem facing Palmer was that there were now too many gaps. Palmer read the reports again. This time he spotted what he was looking for. A single reference to a meal, but it was for the wrong night. So he still could not place her on the night of the fatal incident. It was a start point though, but sadly the report failed to mention the restaurant. Palmer held on to this morsel of information.

Now his client was under arrest, and her solicitor had disappeared. He picked up the sheet of papers that contained his notes from the computer enquiries and with the fingers of his free hand raked his hair. He recognised the name of his client's partner, but it was surely a coincidence that he had a request for surveillance on a person with the same name.

His years of experience told him that something was wrong, that something didn't fit. Most of all he did not understand why his client should have an apparently perfect recollection of her whereabouts on the 12th June, but could remember nothing about the day itself. It simply made no sense to him. He was still puzzling the information he had to hand when the doorbell sounded. At first he seemed not to have heard it but then, as if in slow motion, he slowly lowered the papers to the desk and walked out into the hallway.

The man at the door was perhaps no more than five foot six inches tall. He was slightly overweight for his height. His face was cheery, and the spectacles that perched on the top of his somewhat red nose were almost comical.

"Damien, me old mate. Gotcha message. Can I come in?" The voice was almost East End but not quite.

"Sure Eddie." The shorter man entered the terraced house and the door was shut firmly. "Thanks for coming over so quickly. See anything outside." The two men sat down in the front room office.

"Nope. I walked up and down a couple of times to be sure. Nobody in their car or hovering. So, what's it all about? You didn't say much in the E-mail."

"I know – I don't know who's listening in these days. Do you remember Jane, Jane Dervan?"

"Jane Dervan, the angel divine?"

"That's the one."

"Yeah. You had something on with her at some point year or so back, didn't you?"

"That's the one. Well I saw her again last night. Then this afternoon I got a phone call telling me she's had an accident and for me to stay away from a case I'm working on. Seems like someone doesn't want me involved. Anyway I called her on the phone but there was no response. To make it worse my client has been arrested and her brief has disappeared."

"No kidding, and what's "is name?"

"Chap called Goodland."

"Not, Goodland of Goodland, Peasbody and Nash?"

"Yes. You've heard of them then?"

"Sure I have. Every fence on the bleeding street's heard of them, and quite a few would just like them to disappear. Right crook's enemy they are. You won't get much sympathy there."

"I'm not after sympathy Eddie, I just want to find out about Jane." His voice was tired and pleading.

"Oh yeah, Jane. What do you want me to do?"

"Leg work Eddie. It's risky but I need someone to go and check out her flat. Someone out there is stirring it and I need to find out why."

"Fair enough. I'll go and check out the flat. Anything else?"

"Wimbledon."

"Wimbledon?" The smaller man almost spat the word out.

"Yeah, Wimbledon, that's where my client lives. Here's the address. Do some asking around and see what you can come up with. Remember we're going back sixteen months now – just before the tennis. Someone may know something – if they do I want to know too. After that I want you to do the same round Jane's address. I haven't seen her for maybe a year, so I need to know who she mixes with – that kind of thing."

"Great! Wimbledon and London. And where will you be keeping warm?" The voice was filled with heavy sarcasm. Eddie knew his old friend too well to know that Palmer would simply sit back, for Palmer had never been one to do that.

"Me. I'll take a trip into Sutton – a few enquiries to make." The men began to walk back towards the hallway as if their conversation would soon be ended.

"Oh, anything of interest?"

"Dunno really, but there are a few names I need to check out."

"Right. You'll be in tomorrow?"

"Yeah. Drop me a line if you hear anything."

"Okay. Until tomorrow then."

"Cheers Eddie." The two men stood at the doorway and as the smaller of them walked down to the pavement Palmer shut the door. It would be another long, late evening, and Palmer had work to do.

The afternoon gloom was already turning into an even gloomier evening and the weak light was faded rapidly as Palmer drove south from his terraced house. The late afternoon traffic was beginning to clog the roads as yet another rush hour loomed. Several times Palmer queued in slow moving lanes of traffic. Passing through the same area of Wimbledon as he had visited the previous evening he continued South through Morden and on into the area of the town of Sutton. His first stop off was a quiet residential road. As he entered the road he noted the metered parking bays and smiled inwardly as he wondered whether anyone would bother to check on the meters in the rapidly advancing evening gloom. He located the house he was after and found a parking bay some fifty yards further on. The road was quiet with little traffic and in a few seconds Palmer had executed a swift "three point turn" manoeuvre, parking the car neatly in the bay so that he could easily watch the house.

He glanced at his watch. It was five thirty. He sat and waited, pretending to read a tabloid newspaper he had brought with him, though all the time his experienced eye was watching the front door of the house. After maybe half an hour his patience was rewarded for the occupant of the house walked down the pavement and let herself into the house. Palmer smiled to himself. The woman was no more than thirty five years old. Although her petite body had been well wrapped up against the night air Palmer had clearly spotted her curly blond hair. He sat back and waited. Now, at least, he knew his target was indoors. It would, he hoped, be only a matter of time before she came out again. He mentally decided to give it until nine o'clock if necessary, and then he would go and make the calls he needed to whilst in the Sutton area.

From his vantage point he watched as other dwellers in the road returned from their day at work. The evening passed slowly. Palmer had never really liked sitting in cars undertaking surveillance operations, but he had little choice tonight. At precisely quarter past eight he observed the light disappear from just inside the house he was watching. A moment later the front door opened and the same woman he had seen earlier reappeared. This time she was definitely not dressed to protect her from the weather. The dark knee length boots looked to be the same that she had worn earlier. Now she was wearing a short, very short, skirt that showed off her stocking clad thighs. The thick coat had been replaced with a figure hugging dark number that seductively showed off the wearer's finer attributes. She walked down the road to where she had left her jet black VW Golf. In a moment the engine purred into life and almost at the same moment she pulled out into the road.

Palmer was ready for her, and counted his blessings that the roads were still quite busy. He pulled out behind her and successfully negotiated the first corner. She seemed preoccupied with something in the car as Palmer attempted to stick to her like glue.

Through the back streets of Sutton and on towards Cheam and Worcester Park they travelled. Every now and then Palmer pulled back in an attempt to make his surveillance less obvious. He knew that the woman would not be expecting him to follow her, but then again it would be better not to arouse too much suspicion – not yet. Quite suddenly the Golf, without indicating, turned off into the drive of a small semi-detached house. As he had been some distance behind her at that point Palmer was able to pull up almost opposite the house, just in time to see the woman standing at the door of the house.

Just as he parked his own car a light came on in the hallway. A moment later the door was opened and a man appeared. Palmer picked out his features in the available light. He was a good deal taller than the woman, probably over six feet. His hair was dark and neat and he had the physique of an athletic person. The two kissed briefly on the doorstep and Palmer was ready with the camera. It was now dark outside and obviously he had not been able to take the picture with the benefit of a flashlight. Palmer had no idea if the photograph would be of any use to him but it was worth the effort.

As the front door closed Palmer saw the occupants move into what was evidently the living room. The thin curtains were drawn but the couple was adequately silhouetted as they clearly embraced. Palmer watched as they held each other closely for several minutes. To him, this was one of the more frustrating elements of his work. If the curtain had been open then he would have got all the evidence he wanted and could have gone home, but as it was he had to wait for what might happen next.

What happened next was entirely predictable. After some ten minutes or so the shadowy forms of the couple disappeared from behind the curtains.

Palmer noted the landing light as it came on, followed several seconds later by the bedroom light. The house was not overlooked and the curtains remained open. After all, the occupants had no reason to suppose that they could be observed, especially as the road was not on a bus route. In fact, opposite the house was a play area, which at that time of night was unoccupied. The single gate in the low fence that was used to keep dogs and other animals out of the play area itself was locked. It took Palmer less than thirty seconds to retrieve the telephoto lens from his brown case and attach it to the front of his camera. It took thirty seconds more to leave the car and leapfrog the low fence. There had been no pedestrian walk down the road since his arrival and to Palmer the opportunity was not to be missed. The slide was partly hidden from the road by some trees in any event and offered the sleuth some protection against observation.

In a few seconds Palmer had climbed the rungs of the ladder and was perched on the very top of the slide. He stood up precariously and found he had a very good view of the bedroom. The light was still on and he had a perfect view of the couple in the room. The woman was undressing, and Palmer watched as she pulled off the two remaining items of clothing. The man was already lying on top of the bed and clearly he was looking forward to what he hoped was about to happen. Through the high-powered lens Palmer had a good view. Click. The sound of the shutter opening and closing was followed by the hum of the automatic winder. As the woman joined the man on the bed Palmer noticed that her head alone was covered by hair. Click.

Palmer watched them as they kissed and caressed each other. He watched as the man massaged the woman's back having previously applied a little liquid from a bottle. Then the woman returned the favour before she rolled over and allowed the man to massage her chest. Under his ministrations her body began to move rhythmically.

For several minutes Palmer watched their antics as their mutual passion increased. He watched as they explored the pleasure of trying numerous positions as they played on the black, silk looking sheets. He watched as their mouths joined in the long, lingering passion of foreplay. He watched as each mouth then took its turn to explore its partner's anatomy.

He watched as they settled for their favourite position with the man crouched dominantly over his quarry. He watched every thrust and withdrawal that took place, the telephoto lens providing him with an embarrassingly detailed view.

He watched as they finished their acts of lovemaking and lay next to each other holding hands. At various points he pressed the little black button on the top of the camera, hoping the activity would be recorded for his client. He watched as the woman replaced her attire and then he climbed back down the ladder on the back of the slide. He noted the time. He had been up there for just over half an hour.

Finally he regained the relative warmth and comfort of his car. There was little point in waiting any longer as he had the evidence he needed, so he started the engine and drove off. Palmer knew from his client what would happen next, and he could clear up the details of that in the morning. For now he had a more pressing engagement, the Cavendish case once again beckoned his attentions. Palmer drove back to Sutton and joined the one-way system that circumnavigates the main shopping area. He drove past the cinema complex and the NCP car park and followed the road round to the right. The road curved round the bottom end of the shopping area and then Palmer parked the car on the left side at the end of a small row of vehicles.

A minute later he was standing outside a block of offices that were shrouded in darkness. He scanned the column of business nameplates by the main door and found what he was looking for. The two names were familiar to him from the list he had compiled earlier. "Zeta Supplies Ltd. (UK)" occupied the offices on the second floor. There was no clue as to the business activities of Zeta and Palmer had no idea what they supplied. The name of the second company gave more clues. The name of "Baker and Derwent" was more familiar to him. A small firm of architects, the name of Baker corresponded to the person who had been found dead in the seat of a smashed BMW. Palmer presumed that the other half of the business partnership had elected to retain the name of his deceased partner in the business name for the sake of familiarity.

Out of habit rather than hope he pushed against the front door. He was not surprised to find that it was firmly locked. It was now quite late and he still had the journey home. There was little more he could do. He had earlier discovered that Cavendish would be brought before the magistrates at three the following afternoon, but it was a formality and the hearing would only last a few minutes. She would be charged and he assumed bail would not be granted. There was little Palmer could do though he would have liked to have talked with his client's solicitor. He looked at his watch. It was just after ten o'clock. Sitting in the driving seat of his car he dialled the solicitor's home number. The phone rang, and rang, but was not answered. Palmer began the journey back to his terraced house, grateful that the traffic was light. As he drove his mind was filled with questions, too many questions and too few answers.

It took nearly an hour to drive back to his home. Once inside Palmer switched off the light that he had habitually left turned on in his office and retired upstairs.

**

Whilst Palmer had been travelling round Sutton, his good friend and colleague Eddie Marston had been extremely busy. He had taken the tube to Green Park and then walked towards the flat where Palmer had stayed the night before. The flats were quiet though some of the occupants were obviously at home judging by the glow of light bulbs. He pressed the buzzer for the flat occupied by Jane Dervan. He received no reply so he picked on the flat that he reckoned would be next door. Again there was no reply, but his third attempt was more successful. The woman's voice was clear and sharp.

"Hello?" Clearly she was not expecting visitors.

"Hi," Eddie began. "I don't know if you can help me but I'm trying to locate a Miss Jane Dervan. I'm told she lives around here."

There was a pause as the woman upstairs decided what to say next. Finally she spoke.

"And you are?"

"Oh, sorry, I'm her brother George. Not that I'm much of a brother. Been out of the country for years and only got back a couple of days ago. Thought I'd look her up but couldn't find her number. I think this is the right address."

"Well, there is a Jane who lives in flat 9 but I don't know her surname." The woman was obviously suspicious and Eddie decided not to push his luck any further.

"Oh. Thanks, I'll try flat 9 then."

"But she's not in, hasn't been back since this morning."

"Oh?" Now it was Eddie's turn to be suspicious.

"Yes. I heard her go out with a gentleman quite early. I was getting ready to leave when I heard a man's footsteps out on the stairs. I knocked on her door about an hour ago and she wasn't back. And she hasn't come in since."

"You're sure?"

"Oh yes. I can hear anyone coming into the flats."

"Okay, thank you, and sorry for troubling you."

The intercom went dead. Eddie looked up at the flat that was shrouded in darkness. It looked for the world as if Jane was not at home.

Eddie made his way back to the tube station and headed for Wimbledon. He hoped that Palmer, who at that time was sitting outside a house in Sutton, was having better fortune. The interminable tube journey down the District Line to Wimbledon finally came to an end. As the train pulled up at the terminus the few remaining passengers spilled out onto the pavement. Eddie made his way to the bus stop and replicated Palmer's journey of the previous evening. The bus was virtually empty and the journey up the hill to Wimbledon Village and the Common was soon complete. Eddie walked briskly towards the block of flats where Helen Cavendish lived. Again he went through the "buzzer on the door" routine. This time, though, the routine resulted in a man's voice.

"Helen Cavendish? And you say you're her brother? You'd better come up. Flat 8, first floor." The voice, despite the interference from the intercom, was refined and strong. The outer door was opened and Eddie entered into the unknown. He half ran up the stairs to the first floor where the middle-aged gentleman was waiting for him at the door to flat 8.

"Eddie, you said wasn't it?" The voice was better bred than it had sounded earlier. The fact that the owner of the voice had a rounded chubby face with a resplendent moustache made Eddie Marston think back to the imagery of the World War 2 flying aces he had watched so much on film as a child. The man was perfect, if the surroundings were not.

"Yes, Edward Cavendish, long lost brother of Helen. You know her?"

"Well, yes, I suppose I do. But look, do come in."

"Thanks." Marston entered the gentleman's flat and was shown into the immaculate lounge.

"Drink? Scotch?"

"Thanks."

"How do you have it?"

"On the rocks or neat."

"Splendid. The only real way you know."

"The only real way for what?"

"The only real way to drink it."

"Oh I see. You said you know Helen. Only I've been trying to get hold of her and I can't find her, but she does live here somewhere, doesn't she?"

"Oh, absolutely, well sort of."

"Please?" Eddie's voice was almost pleading now.

"How do I put this? Hmm," he paused for a moment before continuing. "Well, she lives at number 7. Leastwise she did till about sixteen months ago. A lovely person, she was so friendly, always willing to help. I have this leg thingy which makes getting out a bit tricky when it's cold and wet." He prodded his left leg with a fat finger. "Anyway about sixteen months ago she went through a real character change, like she was a completely different person."

"How do you mean?"

"Well, she stopped being friendly – actually she didn't seem to have the time of day for anyone any more. And she started staying away a lot – hardly ever here. Also there was something else that changed. Seems crazy, but she actually seemed to get shorter by a couple of inches. Must've been a trick of the light. Anyway, she virtually became a recluse after that – wouldn't talk to anyone at all."

"That doesn't sound like Helen."

"No it doesn't, and it certainly wasn't Helen until, well, summer before last. I still hear her occasionally, banging around in her flat sometimes, vacuuming, that sort of thing, but I don't think we've actually talked for about three months now."

"Strange."

"Yes. Anyway she was in yesterday for a bit, and then she went out again quite abruptly. Didn't see her but I heard her slam the door shut, and it's been quiet ever since. Someone came and banged on her door last night but she didn't open it. Which reminds me, I must mention keeping the outer door locked at the residents meeting next week."

"Big problem is it?"

"No, not really, it's just sometimes left open and we get people banging on the flat doors."

"Oh, right. So you don't know where my sister is then?"

"No, I'm afraid not, but she'll be back sometime. She often disappears for several days and then comes back again. Don't know where she goes, but she always comes back."

"Could be a boyfriend perhaps?" Marston thought it worth enquiring.

"Don't think she has one right now. Did have a chap round sometimes up until she changed, but I haven't seen or heard him recently."

"Yeah, she did write and tell me she'd split up with someone a while back come to think of it. Oh

61

well, I'd best be on my way, and thanks for the drink. If you see her in the next few days will you tell her Eddie called to see her?"

"Of course I will. Sure you don't want another drink first?"

"Well..."

"Oh, go on man, one for the road. Gets pretty lonely up here sometimes I can tell you, and it's always nice to have a chat. Your sister for example, what does she do?"

Marston thought quickly and remembered his earlier conversation with Palmer. "She's involved in cosmetics somehow or other. Don't really understand what she does, but it's something to do with supplies. I think she's involved in the selling side of it all, but it's all beyond me I'm afraid."

"Oh." The moustachioed gentleman looked somewhat surprised at this latest revelation. "That's very curious. I'm sure she told me a few months ago that she was involved in computer software. Must have got it wrong, but she looked more like a boffin than a beautician. Still looks can be deceiving."

"No, she was definitely in cosmetics."

The two men continued talking for another half an hour but Eddie had already extracted about as much information as he could from the other gentleman. Finally, and without being rude Eddie glanced at his watch.

"Look, I really do have to go. I've got a trek back to the hotel and it's getting late."

"Oh. Well, if she comes round I'll let her know you called in. Where are you staying?"

"Well actually I'm moving around a bit. I'm off to Germany tomorrow for three days and then

France. Should be back in England next week. I'll try to look her up when I get back."

"Very well then, and thanks for a most interesting chat."

Marston walked back down the flight of stairs and left the flats. His own home was some way away and it took him nearly an hour to reach it. A few miles away Palmer had just reached his own terraced house and retired for the evening.

Chapter 3

The following morning saw Palmer rise early. Before attending to the pressing concerns of the Cavendish case, as he had dubbed it, he had a film to develop. It took him about half an hour and he was nearly finished by the time the sun began its ascent on the horizon. The shots he'd managed to take whilst perched on the top of the slide had proven to be even better than he had dared hope. He had even been tempted to keep some of them.

The female subject was clearly identified in all her natural splendour as was the male subject. The developing complete, Palmer took the prints down to his office. In a couple of minutes the computer was waiting for him to type up the report that would accompany the photographs. It was a detailed report, giving the details of the route the subject had taken from her home to her destination. Palmer relished these kinds of reports and he went to great lengths to describe everything he had observed.

When he had finished, he read the report through twice as it sat on the screen before deciding to print it off. Somewhere in the desk cupboard the printer started to turn the contents of the screen into hard copy. A few minutes later he had created the invoice that would accompany the evidence he had amassed. As the invoice printed on the machine he looked at his watch. He had just over six hours before his client was due in court to be formally charged.

In the hall, a grandfather clock chimed 9 o'clock. Almost immediately the phone rang.

"Damien, it's Eddie, how's tricks."

"Oh, thank God it's you Eddie. Can you come over?"

"Sure. Have I got something to tell you."

"Likewise. See you in say an hour. No make that two, I've got someone to see first."

"Right then, two hours. See you then." With that the line went dead again.

Palmer busied himself around the desk. He collected the photographs and the negatives, his report and the invoice and stuffed the whole lot into a large manila envelope. It took him five minutes to don coat and shoes and then he was on his way. He walked briskly along the leaf-covered pavements till he came to the small but neat offices of "Duggan and Mortimer Architects". He opened the glass front door and went inside. The secretary at the front desk looked up enquiringly as the door opened. Palmer noted that although her computer was on, she had not actually started work. As she looked at him he noticed that it might have been connected with the fact that her bright red nail varnish had not quite dried. Palmer walked to her desk and spoke in hushed tones.

"Robert Mortimer please."

"And who may I say is asking?"

"Palmer, Damien Palmer."

The petite brunette stood up and walked back into the office and knocked on a door that Palmer couldn't quite see. In a moment she returned and beckoned the investigator into the office.

"This way Mr. Palmer."

"Robert, it's good to see you. I have those plans you wanted." Palmer talked brightly, purely for the benefit of the secretary.

"Thanks, Siobhan, could you shut the door please." The secretary duly obliged and Palmer noted that a roller blind on the back of the door had already been lowered to provide some privacy.

Palmer duly accepted the seat that was offered him and watched as his client opened the envelope and removed its contents. He watched as his client began to go pale, and then waited patiently as the report was scrutinised.

"This is a very thorough job, Mr. Palmer, a very thorough job. I am indebted to you for this. Do you know the man, or have you heard of him?"

"No I'm afraid not. I could check him out if you want me to. It would take a day or so, but your instructions were simply to get evidence."

"Yes, quite so, and to think that bitch has been fucking him. No wonder we're bloody struggling. Bound to, when your own wife sleeps with the opposition. Leastwise I know how all our good ideas are being leaked. You really don't know this guy?"

"No, sorry, should I?"

"Well, probably not. He's Simon Derwent, bit of an entrepreneur. Knows how to make a quick buck shall we say. Has a brother, Richard, who's in the same line of business as us. You must have heard of Baker and Derwent?"

"Hmm. Oh yes." Palmer feigned ignorance with professional aplomb. "They're Sutton based, aren't they? Won a major building contract about six months ago. Some revolutionary design technique – could save millions on the construction costs or something, wasn't it?"

"Yes. Well it was our invention, our design. Only the blue prints disappeared about ten months ago and there was no time to reinvent the wheel. Wait till I get home tonight, I'll kill that two faced tart."

Palmer decided that two and two suddenly added up to five and he looked hard at his client, wondering how to approach the next stage of the conversation.

"You said Baker and Derwent?"

"Yeah. You have heard of them, haven't you."

"Not really." Palmer lied. "But wasn't the other partner, Baker, killed in some motor accident some months ago?"

"Murdered more like. I had the greatest respect for John Baker. We were at University together. Almost ended up setting up our own business – shame we didn't. He was as honest as the day was long. This scam wasn't his idea. That's all down to his partner and that brother of his." With that he used his index finger to stab at the male in the nearest picture and by coincidence the finger hit the area of his genitals.

"Look, Mr. Mortimer, can I ask you one big favour? Don't say anything for forty-eight hours. I'll level with you. I'm looking into the Baker thing and it could work out better for you if you say nothing. If as you say you liked John, then just give me forty eight hours – for his sake."

"Forty-eight hours, I don't know, that could be difficult?"

"Why not stay in a hotel or something. Pretend you're away for a couple of days. Please!" Palmer rarely pleaded with any one for assistance and he surprised himself at this request. Somewhere in the depths of his brain things were beginning to add up and he just needed a little bit of time.

"Forty-eight hours, okay then, but it had better be worth it. Look, would you mind holding on to these. Some people round here have slippery fingers and I can't afford for these to go astray."

"Fair enough." With that Palmer walked back to the door and opened it. "And I'll be in touch in a couple of days just to check everything's going smoothly." His mentally rehearsed closing speech was wasted as no one was outside.

Palmer walked back to the secretary's desk and noticed that the computer screen had still not changed.

"Thank you, and I like the nail gloss." He smiled sweetly but falsely at the young woman.

Her reply was lost as he exited the offices and walked back up the street. As he did so, Palmer mused on the latest extraordinary revelations. He mused on the odds a bookie would offer him to have two connected cases going on at the same time. The brown bag swung limply at his side, the brown manila envelope safely inside.

**

Palmer had not been home for more than ten minutes when the front door bell sounded. He opened it and Eddie Marston joined him as they went into the office. For the next half an hour

68

Palmer listened intently as the other man related his story of the previous night. Palmer looked up quizzically when Marston got to the bit about Cavendish changing character abruptly.

"And did he say anything about why he thought she did?"

"No. But I suppose it could have been to do with the accident."

"I doubt it. According to Goodland she's been in cosmetics since leaving school. So I don't know where this computer stuff comes from, but it's worth thinking about. For now though we've got a problem."

"Yeah, what's that?"

"Goodland, her solicitor is missing and I haven't been able to talk to Jane. Are you sure she wasn't in last night?"

"As sure as I can be. The flat was dark, and the person said she'd heard her go out with a chap early that morning."

"So someone must have visited her after I left. I wonder who that might have been? And I wonder where she is?"

"I don't know. Maybe you ought to report it?"

"I can't. Remember the phone call yesterday? But you could!"

"No way, I'm not going nowhere near a cop den. And anyway, chances are if they're watching you, they'll be watching me too by now."

"True. In that case keep your ears open and see if anything turns up. Also can you go to the court this afternoon to hear the committal?"

"Yeah, sure, anything else?"

"I don't think so, not for the moment anyway. I think I might just go back to Sutton and see if I can spot the living partner in Baker and Derwent. I've got the mobile. Ring me if anything comes up. If not, I'll talk to you later on."

"Yeah, okay." Marston put his coat back on and was ushered to the front door. In a moment he was ambling nonchalantly up the road and soon disappeared from Palmer's sight.

Palmer closed the front door and returned to his office. He took a sheet of paper from the top drawer and began to write down a list of the names of the people who might be involved. So far he had only one link. It wasn't much to go on but it was a start. He looked at the list of names he'd compiled. The Bakers were dead, Cavendish was in prison, Mortimer the architect and his wife seemed uninvolved except for the tenuous link that Mortimer had been at University with Baker and he thought that Baker's partner might have stolen some blueprints several months earlier. Finally there was Baker's business partner, the as yet unknown Richard Derwent, and his brother Simon Derwent who seemed to be involved with Mortimer's wife. Palmer decided it would be of interest to know a little more about the Derwent brothers.

Before leaving to drive to Sutton he made a quick enquiry using the laptop and noted down the address associated with the name he'd entered. The journey, though now familiar to him, still took the best part of an hour. Palmer left the car in the NCP car park and went on foot round the corner to the offices of Baker and Derwent. He found, as expected, that the front door was open but decided against entry. Instead he crossed the road and entered the Pizza restaurant that offered both sit down and take-away facilities. He picked the small table nearest to the window and ordered a Pizza.

After about ten minutes the Pizza arrived and Palmer was just about to cut into it when the door of the offices over the road swung open. The camera was almost invisible to an observer but the sound of the winding motor betrayed its location as Palmer reeled off three quick snaps. He knew the camera was perfectly positioned. He'd spent a couple of minutes ensuring that it was while at the same time pretending to search for some papers in the bag. The person walked off towards the High Street and Palmer pretended to concentrate on his lunch.

Less than five minutes later a woman emerged from the building. Palmer stared at the figure, thinking that he had seen her before but unable to be sure. The winding motor on the camera again indicated three snaps had been taken. The same simple procedure was repeated for each of the next three people that left the building.

Finally Palmer paid for the Pizza and left the restaurant. He walked straight into the offices of Baker and Derwent and found exactly what he was wanting. The secretary looked up at him as he entered the offices.

"Hello," she called out, " can I help you?"

"Richard Derwent please."

"I'm sorry, Mr. Derwent has just gone out to lunch."

"Damn. I said I'd try to get here for lunch but I got held up. Do you know where he went?"

"Same place as usual."

"And that would be?"

"Pub on the corner, round there." The woman gesticulated wildly in some vague direction. "You'll find him in the upper bar sitting on his own."

"Thank you, you've been most helpful."

With that Palmer made his farewells and exited the offices. He quickly walked round the corner following the vague direction of the woman's pointing and happened upon the pub she had described. Inside Palmer saw that there were two bars on two levels. The lower level was quite busy whilst the upper level was virtually deserted. At the bar itself on the upper level a lone person sat drinking. Palmer recognised him as the third person to have left the building. He made a note of his observations and left. He walked back to his car, paid the attendant and drove back home. It was a little after two o'clock when he returned and it took him just under the hour to develop the latest reel of film. This time he made prints of the people that had left the building. He took them back down to the office and scrutinised them. One he could identify as being the subject of his journey that morning. The surviving partner of Baker and Derwent was a man who looked older than his forty-five years. His grey hair and overweight structure indicated that he was a man hounded by many worries. The picture of the woman that had attracted his attention lay beside Derwent's. The woman's picture was not particularly clear but Palmer felt that he should have recognised her. He turned to his laptop and made notes. Finally his report of the morning's activities was printed and the details added to the growing case file. Palmer looked at his watch. It was half past three.

At four o'clock the phone rang. It was Marston and he confirmed that Cavendish had been remanded in custody for twenty-four hours, and that she had been charged with murder. Palmer said little and when the conversation ended his face was grim. He looked at the rows of leather bound books as if seeking inspiration before his eye fell casually back to the photographs still lying on his desk. He opened his brown case and withdrew the manila envelope he had been carrying around. He extracted the photographs and selected the one that showed the woman's face with greatest clarity. He used his hands to block out the distractions from the rest of the picture and concentrated on her eyes and nose. He did the same with the picture he'd taken that morning and then sat back. Holding both pictures next to each other a smile came to his face.

"Gotcha." He muttered to the pictures. "Question now is, what were you doing there?"

Palmer knew for certain that Sharon Mortimer worked in Sutton. Of course her beauty parlour was not on the High Street but in a back street in the less opulent part of the town and quite some distance from the offices of Baker and Derwent. Possibly she had gone to the offices to see the brother of her lover, but that didn't make much sense. Palmer felt there must have been a better reason. He just didn't know what it was. He was still contemplating the conundrum when the phone rang.

"Mr. Palmer?" The voice was polite and formal.

"Yes."

73

"Hello. We spoke yesterday. I'm John Nash, a colleague of David Goodland."

"Oh, yes, Mr. Nash, I remember."

"I understand you are doing some work for Mr. Goodland with regards to one of his clients?"

"Helen Cavendish, that's right."

"Well, I've taken over the case. Mr. Goodland appears to have disappeared without trace. I was wondering if you could come to my offices tomorrow morning at ten o'clock for a chat. Obviously I've only just picked up on it all and I need to know how you are getting on as well."

"Ten. That's fine by me." Palmer omitted to say that he was probably being followed. "I have a call to make first, so I may be a few minutes late, but I'll be there as soon as I can. Any news on Miss Cavendish?"

"Yes. I was in the court today. Charged with murder and remanded in custody for twenty-four hours. We'll be presenting an opposition tomorrow. Talk to you about it in the morning. Good bye."

"Good day." Palmer replaced the receiver. He looked again at the pictures and made a decision for the following day.

He turned once again to the lap top computer and a few minutes later had typed in the name of Mortimer and the address in Sutton that he had traced the woman from the previous evening. After a few seconds the screen returned the information he already knew. The only people that lived at the house were Robert and Sharon Mortimer, and no one else. Palmer clicked on another icon and in a moment was searching the details recorded at Company House. He noticed that there was a

Sharon Mortimer registered as a Partner of "The Beauty Centre" whose registered offices were in Sutton. He was not surprised, because it was not news to him, that the other Partner was a certain Helen Cavendish. He printed the details and made a fresh enquiry. Sharon Mortimer was not registered as a Director in any company or linked to any other Partnership. Nor was Cavendish, but Palmer already knew that fact. He turned again to his list of names and drew an arrow between the names of Cavendish and S. Mortimer. On the line he wrote two words, "Bus. Partners". There were still a lot of gaps but Palmer was pleased with the results of the day's work so far. He was curious that Cavendish had not mentioned her business partner, but then again he hadn't asked the question. Anyhow, in all probability it was a red herring, a coincidence that would never have come to light if he had not had the two cases to deal with in the same week. He looked again at the growing pile of photographs and wondered what would transpire next.

It was getting dark now and Palmer looked at the pile of unopened mail that lay neatly on the corner of his desk. Habitually it was the first thing he did in the morning. The bills he put to one side, as they were relatively unimportant. Of more urgent need were the two letters that bore the names of local solicitors. He had been expecting both envelopes and felt guilty that he had not attended to them earlier that day. The first letter contained a request for surveillance. It was not essential that he did this immediately but he knew it needed to be sorted out in the next couple of days. The second was a document that he needed to deliver in person to the recipient. Palmer had never much liked Process Service, it had an unsavoury taste to it. It was not real investigative work. After all, the document had the name and address of the recipient on it. This one, though, Palmer knew had to be attended to immediately. It was an important document and it needed his immediate attention.

He hauled himself into action. He knew the block of flats where the papers had to be delivered and he did not relish the prospect. The flat was listed as number 39, and Palmer knew, because he had already done some work on this case, that it was a long walk up to the flat if the lifts weren't working, which would probably be the case. He drove slowly for about fifteen minutes and parked the car in a side road. His experience told him that if he parked close to the flats he would probably return to find the car had either gone or at least been vandalised. He had dressed the part for this exercise. The faded and ripped jeans, trainers and tatty anorak Palmer had figured would fit perfectly into the surrounds. He was not wrong. As he walked the last half-mile to the tower block he noticed that his attire was very much in keeping with his surrounds. As he walked along the pavement a drunkard ambled out of the shadows and bumped into him.

"Fifty pee for a cuppa, guv?" His drunken voice was heavily slurred.

"Pardon?" The question took Palmer aback.

"Fifty pee for a cuppa, guv?" The question was repeated, though slightly less slurred than in its initial presentation.

"Sorry, mate, haven't got nothing on me." Palmer tried to act the part of a local, though a sober local would not have been fooled.

"You from round here?" The drunk was becoming too interested.

"Yeah, that's right. What's it to you. Now clear off and leave me alone."

"Only wanted a cuppa." The drunk muttered as he turned away from Palmer who walked away from the drunk with a degree of haste. There was a ten feet high wooden fence lining the side of the pavement. Beyond the fence was a wasteland. The building that had been there had been demolished over a year ago, but the plans to build new properties had never come to fruition.

Suddenly Palmer heard the sound of shuffling feet behind him. He half turned, just in time to see the crow bar being lowered towards his shoulders. Palmer ducked and twisted sideways as the crow bar sliced through the air and connected harmlessly with the pavement.

"Bugger." The drunk was not finished yet. As he turned to face his would be assailant, Palmer saw the crazed look in the attacker's eyes. "You're gonna give me the price of a cuppa or else."

The crow bar was already being raised. Palmer watched as the drunk raised the bar to its maximum height. At its highest point the drunk looked particularly precarious, tottering under the weight of the bar. Palmer watched the bar begin its descent. As it did so he took a step backwards and watched as the bar crashed once again into the pavement. As it did so he took two steps forward. He brought his right knee up and made a perfect connection with the drunk's stomach. The drunk lurched backwards under Palmer's knee and fell into the sidewall. He tottered over and lay curled up in a ball. For good measure Palmer picked up the crow bar with a gloved hand and threw it over the wall into the wasteland beyond. The whole action lasted no more than ten seconds.

"No I'm not." Palmer replied, slightly breathless from the exertion. Leaving the drunk lying on the pavement he continued on his way to the flat

He entered the main door to the tower block and noticed that fortunately the lifts were working. He pressed the lift call button and waited. Eventually he heard the lift arrive and the doors were opened. A young girl and boy emerged giggling. The girl looked dishevelled and the top buttons on her blouse were undone.

"Hey mister?" The boy called back. "What are you looking at? Don't you know it's rude to stare?"

Palmer ignored the banter and entered the lift. He pressed the floor number that he wanted and the lift doors started to close.

"Hey mister." He heard the boy call again. "Think she's got big tits?" The young couple laughed again and as the lift doors finally closed Palmer heard a can of some kind hit the outside. The lift began its ascent. Palmer noticed that the lift had a certain pungent air about it. He tried to breathe shallowly to avoid the worst of the smell. Looking around, the lift was filthy. Graffiti covered virtually all the wall spaces. On the back wall a liquid was dribbling onto the floor. Palmer turned away, the stench almost unbearable. The lift seemed to take forever to climb its weary way to the floor that he wanted. Finally the doors opened and Palmer was glad to be out in the corridor. He checked on the flat number just to be sure, and the name.

A short walk led him to the front door of the flat. There was no buzzer so he knocked loudly. After a minute he knocked again. The door had a frosted glass panel that was cracked. The glass covered the middle section of the door.

"All right, all right, I'm coming." The voice from inside was impatient. Almost at the same time as he heard the voice Palmer saw the bulky shape of a somewhat overweight man shuffling his way to the front door. The door opened sufficiently for the man to peer out.

"Mr. Stephanopoulos?" Palmer queried. The door opened further and the bulk of the owner came into view.

"Do I look like some fucking Greek to you?" The accent was pure English and the shape pure obesity.

"No, can't say you do. Someone must've got their wires crossed at the office. If you let me have your name sir I'll make sure it doesn't happen again."

"Brian Simmonds, now clear off and let me get back to the telly." He made as if to shut the door. As he did so Palmer put a foot in the way and also reached into his inside pocket.

"Thank-you, Mr. Simmonds, I'm acting as a bailiff on behalf of Changrove and Dalrymple, Solicitors. I have a writ here which, as you have identified yourself, I now duly serve." Palmer reached out and handed the document to the house owner. The document fell to the ground. "Doesn't matter, the courts still see this as being served. Good day." Palmer withdrew the foot and began to walk back down the corridor to the lifts and stairs. He opted for the stairs and a couple of minutes later had arrived back at ground level. He noted the time and walked back to the car. The drunk had obviously not been badly hurt as he was now nowhere to be seen. Palmer was glad that the visit was over. It was an old trick he had learned many years ago and he always used it whenever he thought the recipient of Process would be difficult. Having already dealt with Simmonds on a different matter several months earlier he knew what he could be like. The trick, as always, had worked.

It was late when Palmer arrived home. After the rigours of the day he parked the car outside his house and then walked back down the street to the pub. He sat there alone for several minutes sipping at a pint of ale. He was well known in the establishment though he only went there a couple of times a week. It wasn't long before he'd started up conversation with some other locals. It was meaningless banter and did little to take his mind off the Cavendish matter. After three pints he said goodnight to the small gathering and walked the hundred yards or so back home.

Chapter 4

The next morning started fine. The cloud and rain of the previous couple of days had vanished, and now a weak wintry sun shone brilliantly in an almost cloudless sky. Palmer had the affidavit ready, the all-important document that attested to him having served the document the previous evening, when he entered the offices of Clarke and Manning. He was a familiar figure in this establishment and it was not uncommon for him to swear up to half a dozen such documents each week.

"Good morning Mr. Palmer, come to do a swear?" The secretary knew Palmer by sight, and could tell that the document he held was for swearing.

"Morning Carol, yes, just the one today." Palmer had been using this firm of solicitors for over three years. The receptionist was a familiar face to him and he had taken to using her first name some time previously, shortly after he had invited her out for an evening, an evening that had been enjoyable and fulfilling for both of them. That had been a couple of years ago. Palmer still remained friends with the woman though they now saw each other only professionally. It was a rule with Palmer that he never dated married women, and when Carol had become engaged some months after their evening out Palmer had, with a degree of regret, withdrawn from the romantic scene.

"Right, I'll see if Mr. Manning is in." The woman pushed a button on the telephone switchboard and in a moment spoke to the person on the other end of the line. After a few seconds she looked up at Palmer who had sat down on one of the visitor's chairs. "Mr. Manning says to go on through."

"Thank you." Palmer stood up and made his way to the office. The process took no more than five minutes to complete and Palmer was soon leaving the building. As he did so he placed the sworn document in the envelope that already contained a covering letter and invoice, and deposited the sealed envelope in the nearest post box. He walked the short distance back home where he collected his brown bag and almost immediately set off for his meeting with John Nash.

Palmer's watch showed the time was five minutes past ten when he entered the premises of Goodland, Peasbody and Nash, solicitors.

"Damien Palmer to see Mr. Nash." Palmer's voice was unhurried and he added a peremptory smile for the benefit of the receptionist who picked up a phone and pressed a button on the console.

"Mr. Palmer's here." There was a pause. "Yes." She replaced the phone and looked at the man standing before her.

"Mr. Nash will be down in a minute. Would you care to take a seat?"

"Thank you." Palmer sat down and looked round the tiny office that doubled up as a reception room and waiting area. Although the solicitor's offices and the waiting room were familiar to Palmer, he nonetheless looked round out of curiosity. There were the usual periodicals and leaflets that you find in such places. The seemingly compulsory pot plant stood on the floor in one corner of the room, occupying far more room than its cause deserved. On a wall a clock recorded the interminable passage of time, each click of the second hand leading remorselessly to the end of another day's work. Palmer heard someone walking down the stairs, but the person passed the room without entering.

He pulled the manila folder out of his briefcase and began examining its contents. It contained the correspondence he had received from Goodland via Cavendish, his own notes and the photographs he'd taken outside the offices of Baker and Derwent. It did not contain the set of photographs that showed Derwent's brother and Sharon Mortimer's steamy sex session. After all, the photographs were highly confidential and totally unconnected with the matter he was now pursuing.

He heard a second, heavier, set of steps outside and in a moment a tall, wiry man sporting a greying beard entered the room. With a good degree of confidence he looked at Palmer who began to stand.

"Mr. Palmer, thank you for coming, I'm John Nash. Shall we go into my office?" Palmer was now standing and the two men shook hands as if they were old friends.

"Good morning." It took the two words for Palmer to mentally assess the solicitor. His conclusion was that this was a complex man. Although familiar with the firm of solicitors, Palmer had only ever previously worked for David Goodland.

"Please follow me." Nash turned and led the way back out of the office, very business-like but not hurried, though he was a busy man, especially as one of his partners had gone missing leaving him an increased workload.

They entered Nash's office and the door was shut. Palmer was offered a chair.

"Tea, Coffee perhaps?" Nash spoke unhurriedly.

"Coffee would be very welcome, thank you." Palmer spoke benignly, watching his host more from curiosity than anything. Palmer had this habit of watching people. He also had a reputation for summing people up from his observations, and his accuracy was uncanny. However, at the moment, he had met his match. He could not quite work out what lay behind the man who called himself Nash.

Nash sat in his swivel chair and pressed a button on the telephone desk set.

"Two coffees please," he spoke when the little red light flashed on the console. "Oh, and Alice, could we have chocolate biscuits too?" His voice faltered for a moment as he made this last request. The momentary change in tone did not go unnoticed by the sleuth.

"Now, Mr. Palmer, we have a situation and I need to get to grips with it. Did I tell you that our client is due back in court this afternoon?" Palmer nodded so the solicitor continued. "Well, from what I've seen and what I heard yesterday I don't think that the police have enough to keep her locked up until the trial. In fact I don't think the CPS will let it go to trial. All they've got is one letter that's typed and unsigned."

"And there is the matter of a credit card being misused a few days after the deaths. Don't forget that." Palmer added, evenly and cautiously.

"Quite so, but that was accepted by all after the inquest as being a case of the handbags being mixed up – perfectly reasonable thing to happen."

"Maybe, but personally it worries me. Like you say there isn't much for the police to hold her on. Unless, of course, they know something we don't."

"Precisely, so I need to mount a strong objection to bail not being granted, and that is what I intend to do, unless you have uncovered anything in the last few days which suggests my client did actually commit the crime she is charged with."

"Well, there are just a couple of things, but it's all very tenuous at the moment." Palmer relaxed in his chair just as there was a knock at the door.

"Come in". Nash called out just as the door opened. "Ah, thank you Alice. Could you hold all calls for me for the next half hour or so? Thank you," he concluded as the not unattractive brunette nodded in deference. She put the tray she had been carrying on Nash's desk and retreated from the room, shutting the door softly behind her.

"And what are these couple of things? Milk, sugar?" Nash continued once the door was shut.

"Milk. No sugar. Well, first off there is the situation regarding Goodland. I have to ask whether his disappearance is coincidental or is it linked to the case?"

"Why should it be linked?"

"Well, it seems too much for it just to be coincidental, unless of course he was involved in some other case where someone would want him out of the way."

"There's nothing that I know of. And I can't for the life of me think why Miss Cavendish would want her own solicitor out of the way. That's a ludicrous idea."

"Very well, but there's been another disappearance that you won't know about yet. I have a lady friend up in London and I visited her just after I'd seen Miss Cavendish. Next day I get a phone call to tell me she has had an accident and that the same will happen to anyone else I involve in this case. Also I was told to stay well away from the police."

"Good God man, you can't do that."

"I have to. I don't know who they are, and that means it could be anyone next time – even your secretary. Though I have to say that I think it's all just to try and frighten me away from the case. It's almost as if someone doesn't want our Miss Cavendish to have an alibi."

Nash went pale but recovered though not before Palmer had noticed his reaction.

"There's something else you ought to know. Just before I got to this lady friend's I tried to phone Goodland. He was not very talkative, and hinted he wasn't alone. Then he said something about it being a bit chilly up here or something. The connection wasn't very good and the line went dead after that. I might have misheard him."

"And have you told the police about this either?"

"No I haven't, but you can when I've gone. In fact it would be helpful to me if we could use your offices for meetings. I'll level with you. Until I know why someone wants Cavendish locked up and out of the way, and without an alibi, I won't feel at all comfortable with this case."

"So you don't want me to apply for bail this afternoon?"

"Well, I'm in two minds. First off if she does get out on bail at least I can talk to her, with your permission of course. That will also mean whoever is trying to keep her locked up is bound to find out. Secondly if you don't make the application she may get suspicious and change briefs, in which case we lose control. I'd rather she was out and perhaps hidden somewhere if that's possible."

"Not easily done I'm afraid. But if I can get her out you could come and talk to her this evening, if that's any good?" Nash was interested to hear what the detective might have to ask his client.

"That would be really useful. There are some questions I need to ask her. They're the kind of questions that rely on other things she says. If it does lead to an alibi then all we have to worry about is why someone wants her locked up. I guess, without an alibi she'll end up being locked away in any case."

"Probably, but don't jump the gun yet."

"I wasn't. Just trying to work out in my own mind why this has got so damned complex. Two days ago I merely had to find out what she was doing on a certain night sixteen months ago."

"I know. Anyway I really must get on, I have to prepare for this afternoon. I'll phone you when we know the situation. Do you have a mobile?"

"Yes," and Palmer quoted the number as Nash wrote it in his desk diary.

"Until later on then, and thank you for coming in."

"It was no trouble at all. Actually it's quite helpful talking things through with someone." Palmer lied, but it was convincing and went undetected by the solicitor. A few minutes later Palmer was walking away from the solicitor's offices. As he walked he mused to himself about the information he had deliberately not divulged. It still intrigued him that Goodland had disappeared, and Palmer felt sure the disappearance was not unconnected with Cavendish. As he walked away from the solicitor's offices he mused on the very different characters of David Goodland and John Nash. More out of interest than anything he had long ago undertaken some research on the firm of solicitors. Peasbody, Graham J., was the senior partner. Actually, until about five years earlier the firm had been called Peasbody and Associates. Then the well-heeled Nash and Goodland had graduated and qualified to practice and had bought their way into the firm. Coming from the same law school their friendship had begun early in their training. It was almost inevitable that after a few years the somewhat older Graham J. Peasbody had taken semi-retirement, leaving the daily business to the two younger, and very capable, men.

Now, as he walked away from the solicitor's offices, Palmer knew he had a very different meeting to undertake. It was the kind of meeting that any private investigator should be able to undertake without undue concern, and ignoring the intrigue that lay ahead, Palmer felt confident that it was a meeting he should look forward to.

He reached his car and began the journey once again into Sutton. The late morning traffic was light and he progressed well. As he journeyed he pondered in his mind how best to tackle the next item on his agenda for the day.

**

The Beauty Centre was a grand title for the small back street shop that Palmer passed a little after noon. The shop itself was externally emaciated, in desperate need of a good clean and a coat of paint. The shop sign, which was not hung entirely on the level, was the only evidence of any work having been done to the outside of the building in a very long time. Palmer drove past looking for somewhere to park. The road was lined with parking bays most of which were empty. Palmer slowed to look at the little plaques that were posted at intervals beside the bays. He soon saw the reason for the scarcity of parked cars. The bays were for permit holders only, and as he was not a permit holder he drove past.

Finally Palmer found a place to park and having secured his vehicle and paid for a couple of hours he made his way back to the shop he had driven past a few minutes earlier. As he approached the shop he observed just how poorly maintained the exterior was. He hesitated whilst still some way down the road. There was no sign of life. No lights were on inside the building and he began to wonder if his journey had been wasted. He kept on walking having decided it would be wise to try the front door at least, seeing as he was in the area. Just as he was approaching the entrance the door opened. A woman appeared in the open doorway and Palmer instantly recognised her. He approached the woman briskly.

"Sorry to trouble you but I'm looking for a Mrs. Mortimer," he enquired of the woman. His voice was deliberately feigned as well bred. "I understand she works around here."

"You understand well. In fact she works right here, but she's on her lunch break now."

"Oh, I see. Well it was rather important. What time will she be back."

"Depends. Who's asking?"

"Sorry, most remiss of me, my name's Brian Clarke."

"Does Mrs. Mortimer know you?"

"I doubt it, but actually it's all about a business colleague that I need to speak to her about. When did you say she'd be back?"

"I didn't say when, but it would be in about an hour's time I'd say. Of course, if you want you can talk to her while she's having lunch."

"I can?"

"Yes. I'm Sharon Mortimer. Shall we take a walk? Who was it you wanted to speak to me about?"

"Mrs. Mortimer, how very nice to meet you," Palmer continued with a somewhat effusive tone in his voice. "You should know straight off that I'm an investigator – one of those awful chaps that snoops around and things." Palmer had started with a posh voice and he continued with it now.

"An investigator, how curious! What kind of an investigator are you?"

"A Private Investigator, actually."

"A Private Investigator, and how on earth can I help you?"

"Helen Cavendish." The woman stopped walking and Palmer stopped with her. "She is your business partner isn't she?"

"She is. Why on earth do you want to talk to me about her?" The woman's voice sounded slightly shaky at this latest revelation.

"It's all very simple really. I had a phone call a day or two ago asking me to locate her – some solicitor needs to talk to her – a legacy I believe. Anyway I did some asking round and bingo, I ended up at your shop."

"Our shop, actually, but Helen, the beneficiary of a legacy?" If Mortimer were not surprised she was acting her part well. "It can't be. She doesn't have any relatives – well, none that I know of."

"It might not be a relative – could be, say, an old school chum. I don't know to be honest."

"Oh I see. So how can I help you?"

"Well, I was hoping you'd know where she is, being her partner. Only I've spent two evenings sat outside her home and she hasn't been there and I have to find her fairly quickly."

"Not at home, you say. Come, do you fancy a pint?" The woman had started walking again some moments earlier and they were now standing outside a small grey building that boasted a pub sign.

"That's a great idea – but I insist that I pay – well actually it will go on expenses."

"Fair enough – you pay." The two people went into the building and in a few minutes were sat in an isolated corner with their drinks.

"Now, where were you?" The woman spoke after sipping her cider.

"Sat outside her flat, but she wasn't at home at all. Or at least she wasn't answering the doorbell, or her phone, and I didn't see her go out."

"Oh, I see. Well, the truth is I don't actually see much of her these days. Haven't done really since, let me see, about sixteen months ago. There was some kind of incident or something and since then she hasn't really been that interested in the business, if that isn't being too unkind on the poor woman. Kind of a sleeping partner if you like."

"So, what else does she do?"

"Nothing as far as I know. I said she's sleeping but actually I suppose she just spends virtually all her time away attracting new customers – it's what she's good at. I tend to do the beauty bit while she gets the customers. She's good at marketing and all that stuff, but she hasn't got a clue when it comes to massage and beauty therapy. So all in all our little arrangement works quite well really."

"Oh I see." Palmer lingered as he downed another mouthful of the ale. "So you don't really know where she might be then."

"Not really, not anymore."

"Sorry, I don't understand."

"Well, I don't really like to mention it to a stranger, but she's changed. I mean, take a couple of years back and we were the best of mates – virtually knew each other's every move, boyfriends inside legs, bedroom antics, all that kind of thing.

92

Then there was this incident about sixteen months ago I suppose, and since then she's been different. Like she's a different person. She even changed her hairstyle, cut it short and also she changed the kind of clothes she wore. Went from being very relaxed and informal to wearing trouser suits and the like. Used to wear trainers, then went to wearing high heels, that kind of thing."

"I get the picture. And I'll bet she stopped being so friendly."

"You bet she did. Won't talk about anything these days, that's when I do see her. Frankly I doubt I'd know if she'd got a new boyfriend, or if she'd moved home. She must have taken a knock on the head or something and I'm not kidding, her whole personality changed, almost overnight. Come to think of it, she went away for about a week, and when she came back there'd been some kind of incident and she'd completely changed. I can't remember all the details, it was just one of those things that happen from time to time."

"Well, of course it could be something to do with the incident."

"Nah. She wasn't involved. Not directly anyway. From what I can remember it's something like she had a cousin killed in a road crash and she had to identify the body. Okay so it's upsetting, but you don't change, not for a cousin, especially when they didn't see each other very often."

"And you are sure of that?"

"Yeah. She talked about everything before that incident. She had a really nice boyfriend at the time I recall. Smart young Yuppie type, loads of money and a big car. Spent a fortune at the Centre. So she

93

told me, they were almost engaged. That was before the incident. After that incident though I never saw or heard of him again."

"I see. Anyway, just when did you last see Miss Cavendish?"

"Ooh, let me see now. Not this week. Previous one. No, and it wasn't the one before that because I was away and we had to get someone in to cover. So, must be about four weeks ago I should think."

"Seems a long time ago."

"Yeah, but that's not unusual, well not since the incident. I told you I hardly ever see her, she just does her own thing most of the time. All I care about is the clients keep on coming in on her personal recommendation, so I know she hasn't given up on me completely."

"There's no chance she has other work elsewhere, is there? Or someone who might know of her whereabouts?" Palmer observed Mortimer very closely as he asked the question, though he would not have had to have been in MENSA to have noticed the way she paused and bit her lip as if deciding whether or not to reveal something.

"I doubt it," she said after a moment. "Another drink?" The woman raised the query as she put her empty glass back on the table.

"Good idea, look, allow me – same again?"

"Fair enough."

Palmer took the empty glasses back to the bar and ordered refills. As he did so, the woman rearranged her attire and added another layer of lip-gloss to her already brightly rouged lips. Palmer returned with the drinks.

"Do you come here often? He enquired as he placed the glasses on the table.

"Fairly often I suppose. About once or twice a week I should think. Why?" Her voice was not concerned, just curious.

"Oh, no specific reason, now, where were we? She has no other work. What exactly do you do?" Palmer looked at the woman with a degree of amicability and feigned interest.

"I'm a beautician. I work mainly with the ladies, facials, toning, nails, massage, that kind of thing."

"I don't suppose you get many male customers?" His question was meant to be polite but it resulted in an intriguing reaction.

"Actually, we do. We have quite a large male client list, many of them are regulars."

"Really. I never sort of put beauty treatments and being a man together – seems somewhat incongruous."

"Why should it?"

"Don't know really. Just never thought about it I suppose. So what do you do for the men."

"It's similar to the ladies treatments really. Facial and neck massage, nail treatments, stress relief, scalp treatment, and so on.

"Sounds like it must be fun."

"Well, seeing as many of our clients come back time and again it must be good for them. You should give it a try."

"Me. I doubt that I could afford it."

"You'd be surprised. Look, what if I offered you a free facial massage. If you liked it we could book you in for something else in a few days' time and you could tell me if you've found my partner. Actually, if you do find her could you tell her I need her to sign some paperwork for the taxman? It's getting urgent"

"Of course I will. As for today, I am a bit pushed for time."

"Nonsense. It will only take twenty minutes, and you'll go out feeling like a new man." Mortimer smiled sweetly and as Palmer looked into her eyes he could not help but recall the pictures he had taken of her.

"Hmm. I'm not sure."

"Oh, go on. I've got half an hour before my next customer and you've got such a nice face." Mortimer continued to smile as she looked intently at Palmer's face. Finally his resolve weakened.

"Well, if you're sure."

"Just so long as you come back for something else another time." Mortimer licked her lips suggestively but her actions seemingly went unnoticed by Palmer as he finished off the remains of his second pint of ale.

A few minutes later they walked back to the shop and the woman unlocked the door. As they entered the building Palmer was taken aback by the contrast. Just as the outside was in desperate need of attention, so the inside was immaculate. Modern furnishings and crystal white tiles that glistened in the soft light greeted him as the woman turned on the lights. The salon consisted of a waiting area and reception room. The waiting room was beautifully decorated in relaxing pastel tones, with sumptuous chairs upholstered in the softest leather. A neat pine coffee table occupied the centre of the room. On it, neatly arranged, were the almost predictable magazines and, miraculously, a copy of the current day's Times newspaper. Beyond the door from the waiting room lay the treatment areas. Three separate cubicles, each a separate room and each self-contained, greeted Palmer as he was shown through from the reception area.

"So business is good then. You'd never have thought it from the outside."

"You mean looks can be deceiving?" The woman smiled.

"Couldn't put it better. This is amazing."

"That's what they all say. Actually we have a lot of hi tech stuff in here and we decided it was probably better protected by leaving the outside as it is – kinds of makes people believe there'll be nothing worth pinching inside."

"True. But this is quite amazing." Palmer was completely overawed by the luxury of the room in which he now sat.

"Feel free to choose some music from the selection over there. Normally we offer our clients a drink, but as you're driving and have already been to the pub I think I'll just offer you tea or coffee."

"Coffee please, white no sugar." The woman left the cubicle for a moment and Palmer selected a CD to play. After a few moments the strains of a string quartet softly pervaded the peacefulness of the room. Palmer sat back in the chair and began to relax. As he did so, he felt the tension in his neck begin to subside, and for the first time that day he began to unwind. He had been relaxing for nearly five minutes when Sharon Mortimer returned. He started to straighten up but she motioned to him not to move.

"Coffee. Ah, Mozart, very relaxing. Now the coffee is hot so if you'd like to lie back in the chair and relax we'll make a start. Palmer did as he was asked and in a few moments, to the gentle strains of the violin concerto his mind began to drift away as he relaxed.

"Now, the lotion we use is a little cold to the touch but it will make you feel great."

Palmer was relaxed and not really listening. He felt the cream being applied to his face. He felt the fingers gently massage it into every pore as he lay there and was lulled by the violins. As he lay there he remembered the evening before last. He remembered how this same woman who was now touching him had been touching someone else. He remembered how the same fingers that were now massaging the cream into his face had rubbed oil into that other person's body. He remembered how that other person had become aroused by her ministrations and he remembered how it had led to the frenetic sexual activity that had ensued.

As he felt the fingers massage his face as they played, seemingly in rhythm to the violins, with his bone structures he too began to drift off into the realms of sexual arousal. As he did so he was once again perched on the top of the children's slide, once again with his camera providing him with a close up view of the masseuse and her lover.

Once again he could see how she caressed her partner, the long, slender fingers, gently yet firmly massaging the liquid into first his back and then his stomach, before moving on to his genitals. He was once again able to see the precise effect she was having on her partner. It was tantalising to see him lying there almost at her mercy as she squeezed and teased him to attention, as she stroked him until he was literally throbbing from her ministrations. As he watched from the top of the slide he now put himself in her partner's place. He could feel her hands gently massaging the skin around his eyes. He began to long for her to move elsewhere.

Suddenly he became aware of what was happening and his mind kicked into gear. He hoped his feelings had gone unnoticed and he longed for his desires to subside.

"Relax. It's not wrong to feel good about yourself for a few minutes. You're very tense, and nervous. Just relax. I've nearly finished."

Palmer relaxed again, though his manhood continued to remain undiminished. He felt the pads of cotton wool being used to gently lift the cream from his face. Then he felt the cleanser working deep into his flesh. It felt good and his face felt clean, really clean. Surprisingly he felt relaxed, or at least his face did.

"Now, you can enjoy the coffee, and tell me what it was like."

Palmer took the cup and sipped the coffee. "Actually it was very pleasant, very nice indeed." He didn't go into the details of the pictures that had been conjured up in his mind as she had been attending to the massage. "Very relaxing, and if I might say, you are very professional."

"That's kind of you to say that. Now, I must just go and get you one of our brochures, so you can decide what you'd like next time, and then we must book you in."

"Next time?"

"Yes. Our little bargain, remember? You get to see what it was like and then you come again as a paying customer." Her voice was soft and teasing.

"Oh. Well, how about some time next week. I don't have my diary on me, but what about Wednesday, I know I'm free then."

"Morning or afternoon?"

"Afternoon preferably."

"Hang on a tick and I'll check." She disappeared for a minute to return with a well-worn and well-filled appointment book. "Say four o'clock? She questioned.

"Four is fine. What do you suggest?"

"How about this again and then perhaps some nail treatment?"

"Sounds good to me." Palmer had finished the coffee.

"That is unless there is anything else I can do for you?"

Palmer had started to walk towards the cubicle's door but stopped as he heard the question.

"What kind of thing did you have in mind?"

"Oh, that's up to you, but I do offer a comprehensive list of services to all our best male clients, if you understand what I mean Mr. Clarke."

"Interesting." Palmer lied but did not want to offend the woman. He was also slightly concerned that he might once again recall the bedroom scene of a few days ago and that the effects would be very evident now he was standing. "I'll think about it. Until next time."

He smiled carefully as he edged out of the cubicle and walked back through the reception area and out of the shop. He noticed that a middle-aged woman was sitting in the reception area and as he walked back to the car he mused to himself about the kind of treatments she might be about to receive. He also wondered how he would cope with the appointment the following week. It was only a short walk back to the car but Palmer knew he had time to spare on the metre. Instead of walking straight back he decided to walk round for a few minutes. He turned left out of the shop and walked down the road. He'd walked maybe fifty metres when he came across a small, dark coloured car. Palmer knew that hundreds, if not thousands of such cars existed in London alone, and he walked past without taking too much notice. He walked a further fifty metres and crossed the road before turning back. As he did so he noticed that the car was empty. Clearly, he told himself, he was becoming paranoid over small, dark, cars. And yet, it seemed uncomfortably familiar to him. As he passed the car he made a mental note of the Index Number. He walked slowly past The Beauty Centre. There was no further activity and no one else was in the street. Finally Palmer made his way back to his car, still undecided about the appointment he had made for the following week.

Chapter 5

Palmer extracted his car from the car park and joined the one-way system that surrounds Sutton's main shopping area. He noted that it was a little after two in the afternoon and made a mental note that he now had at least a couple of hours to kill. After all, Cavendish was not due back in court until three. It would be at least quarter past, and more likely half past, before she'd know if she had got bail, and then it would take Nash some time to firstly phone him, and then to get the client back to the solicitor's offices. So Palmer figured he had at least two hours. He also figured that it would be pointless to go all the way home, only to have to go out again, if Nash was right. There also wasn't much in the way of work that he could do in the Sutton area.

It was a big question, whether Nash was right. Palmer was not familiar with the legal skills of John Nash. Indeed, his only involvement with the firm of Goodland, Peasbody and Nash, had been through David Goodland. A relationship that had begun some three years previously when Palmer had sent the solicitors a brochure outlining the services that he could offer them. Evidently it had been Goodland who had received the brochure, and indeed it had been several months before Palmer had been contacted. Then, as he recalled, it had been to serve a simple document on some unfortunate person. It was a simple enough task, and one that Palmer accomplished easily.

Time had shown it had been a test case as the firm of solicitors had returned to him often, and indeed David Goodland now held a stock of Palmer's business cards for introductory purposes. Over the years Goodland had provided Palmer with a steady, if relatively mundane, stream of work, and so the professional relationship had developed. Now though, Palmer was faced with a different partner, who doubtless had different skills to Goodland, and a different approach to the use of private investigators. Time alone would tell whether he would find John Nash to be as equable to work with as he had found Goodland to be. As he mused over his first encounters with the firm of solicitors Palmer also decided how he should spend the next few hours.

Palmer disliked these times, the lull periods as he called them. He disliked them even more when he found them taking place in the middle of a case, such as was happening now. Palmer was one of those people who liked to see a task through from beginning to end with as little interference as possible. It was a subject of some mirth amongst his friends that he could talk for hours on end about the merits of concentrating on one task at a time. Indeed his earlier careers had focused much on that way of training the mind. It was, therefore, not surprising that the detective found it frustrating to be unable to progress a task that he was involved with. Palmer had also read much on handling stress and anxiety and he knew that this frustration made him tense. It always did, and as he drove the car now, the frustration at not being able to make progress, began to seep into his mind. From his mind it seeped into his neck muscles and his shoulders. He shrugged his shoulders and rolled them to release the tension as he always did in these moments, and as always his actions had little effect. Deep inside him he knew that the best way of releasing the tension was to be able to get back on with the case. The only trouble was the two hours he still had to wait before he could meet Cavendish.

Consequently, as Palmer drove along killing time, whatever beneficial effects he had received from the massage were soon lost. He turned right on the one-way system and passed the offices of "Baker and Derwent". He continued round the one-way system until he was heading towards Cheam Village. As he neared the village he mused to himself what it must have been like to live round this area fifty years ago.

There would certainly have been fewer shops, although many of the more antiquated buildings were clearly relics from before that time. The more modern supermarket and car parks would certainly not have existed, and Palmer recalled some old pictures of the village that showed the streets as having been little more than dirt tracks, with gaslights at infrequent intervals. Palmer could almost imagine the drays passing down the tracks, a far cry from the motorised transport that clogged the narrow streets of today.

At the village he turned right and headed for North Cheam. That part of the journey took just a few minutes, and after turning left at the main lights he arrived at the park. The car park was relatively empty and, mercifully, there were no small, dark cars to fuel his paranoia. Palmer was glad of his choice. He parked up and began to stroll out over the green parkland grass. He walked slowly, weighing up in his mind what he had discovered to date. It was not actually progressing the case, but the exercise and the fact that he was using his mind on the case helped him to relax. The air was cool and with the clear sky Palmer figured that the first frosts of winter would not be far away. He walked briskly in the weak October sunlight, briskly enough to keep warm. As he walked, he applied his thoughts to the case.

His mind went over the conversation he'd had with Marston about Cavendish's neighbour. The old man, evidently ex-army or something similar, seemed quite convinced that something had happened to Cavendish some sixteen months ago. Could her character change, Palmer wondered, be linked to the tragic death of Sam Baker? Would such an event cause such a change as to be noticed by a neighbour? Or perhaps, Palmer wondered, did the old boy have a soft spot for her and he was a bit miffed that she was seeing less of him? Palmer had to concede that either possibility held water. It was just a question of which one held the most.

Then his mind turned to his chat with Sharon Mortimer. There was at least consistency in the stories. Cavendish had indeed seemed to change shortly after the accident. It made little sense to him, and Palmer could not understand how someone's behaviour could change so abruptly.

As he strolled his mind thought back to the conversation he'd had with Mortimer. He tried to work out where she fitted into the situation, other than just being Cavendish's partner. It seemed unlikely that she did so. After all she had been helpful and friendly. Not only that but she was a damned good masseuse. Palmer reasoned that if Mortimer was part of the case, then she would surely have been less helpful, perhaps even evasive. Yet Palmer had felt very strongly that she was being open and honest with what she had said. Palmer thought back to the massage and the effects that she had had on his body. It was a shame that such a skilled set of hands were involved with the likes of Simon Derwent. Palmer had done some research on Derwent and had discovered some unsavoury aspects to the man's life.

There were the references as a youth to numerous offences. Okay, perhaps Palmer should not have been able to access such information, but he had the key and used it rarely. This was one of those rare occasions when Palmer considered the risks justifiable. With the opening up of information on the Internet, Palmer had contacts to provide him with the information he needed in a fraction of the time it would take to obtain that information using more conventional methods of detection.

Then there were the references to being involved in drugs and also supposed links to the underworld. It seemed that Simon Derwent had a past to be reckoned with. Yet for all that, Palmer was puzzled as to how he had met Sharon Mortimer. Perhaps it had been at a business function. After all, Sharon Mortimer's husband was in the same line of business as Derwent's brother, the Derwent in Baker and Derwent. It seemed a possibility, though unlikely. Perhaps Derwent had simply strolled into The Beauty Centre, but again it seemed unlikely, unless there was something more sinister happening at the place than had been evident when Palmer had visited it a few minutes ago. Palmer dismissed this thought. After all Sharon Mortimer may have been good at what she did but she certainly did not come across as a gangster's moll. Yet, Palmer conceded, she was having an affair with a supposed gangster.

As he strolled Palmer began once again to envy the man he'd seen her in bed with a couple of evenings ago. He started to remember the pictures he'd taken of the bedroom. He started to warm at the thought of becoming more acquainted with the woman the following week. After all, he considered he was still relatively fit for his age, and being a single man he occasionally needed to find comfort somewhere, although his relationship with Karen Shaw had been developing reasonably well over the past couple of months, and only when she was unavailable for a period of time, did his thoughts for others return.

He remembered the pictures he'd taken a couple of nights ago and thought how good Sharon Mortimer had looked through the telephoto lens as her breasts had responded to the man's touch when he had massaged them. It made him warm. His mind dwelled on the pictures until he had walked completely round the pond, following the somewhat muddy track that had been taken by countless people over the past few years.

Once he reached the end of the pond, he allowed his mind to drift to the reaction from her husband when he'd shown him the photographs. It was what he had come to expect from such situations. The anger was genuine enough, as were the assertions that had been made. And then, as he softly cursed himself, Palmer found the connection he was seeking, the very thing that linked Mortimer to the whole case.

In the same moment, Palmer realised that he would have to be very careful from now on. There were people he needed to talk to, oh so very carefully. He began to formulate in his mind the kinds of questions he would need to ask them. He even began to guess at the possible replies. Finally, the game of mind chess that he was playing became too complex for him and he had to give up. He had now walked in a loop round a large part of the park and he had once again happened upon the car park. Just as the car park came into sight Palmer heard his mobile phone ring in his coat pocket.

"Hello. Yes Damien Palmer speaking." A pause while he listened to the voice at the other end of the line. "Four-thirty. That's fine by me. See you there. Goodbye."

Palmer replaced the phone in his pocket and with a more purposeful stride walked back to the car. As he approached the car he became aware of a small, dark car, parked at the other end of the car park. It looked vaguely familiar to him, and it also looked empty. Palmer shrugged off his feelings as advancing paranoia and continued to unlock his car. He sat in the driver's seat and reached into his brown top-opening briefcase. He pulled out the diary and found the number he wanted. In a moment he had dialled the number and spoke for a couple of minutes to someone at the other end. From outside the car his conversation was singularly unanimated. Palmer made no gestures but sat quite still, all the time keeping a cautious eye on the small, dark, car at the other end of the car park. Finally he replaced the phone in his pocket and started the engine.

The car joined the main road a moment later and began to retrace its route back to Cheam and then Sutton. In less than five minutes Palmer was back on the one-way system passing behind Sutton High Street. The traffic system around Sutton has been designed to keep as many vehicles as possible out of the main High Street. Indeed for large periods of time the entire street is entirely given over to pedestrians. The one-way system is efficient and modern and the various sets of traffic lights work together to ensure the flow of traffic into and out of the area is kept as smooth as possible.

Halfway along the road behind the main shopping area is a set of traffic lights marking the pedestrian crossing that links the cinema complex with the main shopping centre.

Palmer was travelling at nearly forty miles an hour in the steady flow of afternoon traffic when the lights began to change. As he registered the amber light so he pressed the brake pedal. The car started to slow but not quickly enough. He plunged the brake pedal to the floor but the car continued to refuse to come to a halt. He was on the left side of the road, and he noticed the teenager on the right side start to walk out into the road. He continued to pump the pedal furiously but to no avail. He suddenly realised that there was no way he could stop in time. With genuine fear he noticed that the teenager was almost halfway across the road.

Almost too late he pressed the centre of the steering wheel, sounding the car's horn.

In that seemingly slow motion that occurs when an accident is imminent Palmer saw how close the teenager was. He could almost count the buttons on her coat. In fact the motion was so slow that he could almost reach out and measure the length of her long auburn hair. He could see the look of sheer horror in her eyes as she half turned to face the vehicle that would not stop. He saw her mouth open a fraction as if she was about to yell, and in the slowness of the motion he could almost count her perfect white teeth. It seemed strange in that moment of slow motion, that interminable moment leading up to the inevitable conclusion, that such an innocent and flawless person as this teenager should be maimed, disfigured, crippled, or even killed, by the car that would not stop.

Suddenly, just when there should have been the sound of impact as flesh and coat met with buckling metal and glass, the motion returned to normal. Somehow, maybe through the teenager taking a step backwards, or maybe through sheer luck, the teenager failed to make contact. The car passed by the girl with the smallest of margins.

In actual fact, the traffic light was still amber as he crossed the line in the road. With Palmer still pumping the brake pedal the car continued, the brakes having virtually no effect. As the motion returned to normal, Palmer reacted to the situation and reached for the handbrake. As he yanked it upwards the car slowed, at first painfully slowly, but within a matter of metres it had slowed significantly. Finally the car came to a halt on the left side of the road and Palmer sat there as the cold beads of perspiration continued to form on his forehead.

A moment later he was out of the car and turned to look up the street. The street was empty. It was as if the teenager had never been there, yet her picture of horror was still playing on Palmer's mind. He returned to the front of the car and examined the near side wheel. Bending down and reaching behind the wheel he felt for the point where the brake's hydraulic connection was. He withdrew his fingers after a few seconds and sniffed at the oily liquid that covered his fingertips.

"Damn," he cursed softly to himself, "brake fluid. Someone's been playing games." Palmer knew there was a garage just around the corner and that with luck an old friend there might be able to fix the problem. So with infinite care he restarted the engine and drove the hundred metres or so to the garage. The car limped into the garage's driveway and Palmer pulled the handbrake to stop it. As he did so a familiar face came out of the up and over garage to see whom the visitor was.

"Damien." The mechanic came forward to greet the car driver. "An unexpected visit old chap, how are you?"

"I'm not so bad Pete. I was in the area so I thought I'd pop in and see how you are."

"I'm not so bad myself. Keeping busy as usual. And you?"

"Yeah, I'm quite busy. Actually I've got a bit of a problem. This old crate is playing up a bit – brakes seem a bit wobbly. Could you give it a check for me."

"Sure. Been keeping my eye open for that car you asked me to look out for. Not heard anything yet, but it could've just disappeared."

"Yeah, you're probably right. Been a month or so now hasn't it. Something would have shown up by now."

"Yeah, you never did tell me what it was all about."

"Didn't I?" Palmer knew full well that he had shared as little about the car he was looking for as he could, but he feigned surprise at the question that was being asked.

"Christ." The mechanic had bent down and looked under Palmer's car.

"What?" Palmer bent down in feigned ignorance.

"Your hose nuts are loose."

"Meaning?"

"Somebody's tampered with your brakes."

"Or they worked loose?" Palmer's attempts to make light of the situation went un-rewarded.

"Nah. They've been loosened and the pipe pulled back to give a leak. Slowly the fluid leaks away and then suddenly you haven't got any brakes. You say they're a bit mushy. I say they don't bleeding work. Not without fluid they don't."

"Can you fix it for me? I'll pay you."

"Yeah, I should think so. Take about ten minutes. Give us a hand into the garage with it."

Together they pushed the car into the garage, until it stood over the inspection pit. The mechanic climbed down the steps into the pit and with an arc light made a more detailed examination.

"Don't look like they cut the pipe, just loosened the end. Very clever that is. Makes it look more like an accident rather than deliberate. Silly buggers though shouldn't have pulled the pipe back. You can see the score marks on the pipe where it's scratched against the locking ring. They're feint but a dead giveaway. If they'd just loosened the nuts the fluid would still have leaked away. Might've taken a bit longer but the effect would've been the same. Some amateurs I'd say."

"Or pros wanting us to think they're amateurs." Palmer interjected, glad that this mechanic was a friend not an enemy.

"Yeah, could be. Anyway you were about to tell me about that car you was after."

"Was I. Oh well, it's a month ago so it probably doesn't matter now."

Palmer went on to relate the events of about a month ago. He'd had a busy week and it was a Friday. There'd been a message on his answer phone when he'd got in from some job or other. Karen had called him during the day to say that she had a free evening if he wanted to meet up. He'd phoned her back and they made arrangements.

He'd gone and picked her up and then they'd spent a very pleasant evening together having a meal and then going to the cinema watching some adult film. It had put them both in the right mood and to cut a long story short he'd ended up back at her place. She was a fairly attractive woman and she'd used her feminine charms on him. Palmer did not tell the mechanic his precise feelings for Karen Shaw, and nor did he tell the mechanic exactly what those feminine charms had entailed. Instead he went quiet for a few moments as the memories of the evening came back to him.

Karen had always been a very warm and friendly person and had spent much of the adult movie telling Palmer what she wanted to do for him later on that evening. Indeed, during the movie he had felt the warmth of her hand on his knee. He had tried to concentrate on the thin plot of the film as her hand had moved towards his stomach. He had felt her caresses as she had whispered in his ear.

Then they had got back to her place. Although it was a modest two-bedroom apartment it was, nonetheless, well furnished, clean and homely. On entering the flat the woman had left Palmer in the lounge and gone to the bedroom. She had returned in a moment and Palmer had appreciated her sexual charms that were barely covered by the thin material of the black nightdress. Clearly she knew what she wanted and Palmer was happy to oblige.

"Now, darling, you need to relax and I have just the thing for you." She led him into the bedroom and helped him out of his clothes until he was wearing only his boxer shorts. "Now lie down and relax."

He'd heard that same phrase before earlier today but then, a month ago, he had not been unwilling and was glad of the attention being paid to him. Her fingers were strong yet soft as they had gently massaged the tension out of his neck. She had knelt beside him dressed only in the black silk nightdress. Her full breasts and the dark surrounds of her nipples were clearly visible through the flimsy material. Palmer though was lying face down as she massaged his back and could not see her nipples stiffen and protrude from under the material as she gently massaged his neck. Had he been able to see he would have realised that Karen was becoming turned on by what she was doing. He remembered how she had moved down his spine with slow, soft, rhythmical movements.

He remembered how, after a while, she had asked him to turn over and had then repeated the same massage on his front. As he turned over Palmer became aware of the arousing effect that massaging him was having on the woman. It had a similar effect on him.

As the effect spread from woman to man so the boxer shorts took on a new shape, a shape that did not go unnoticed by the woman. With a tender yet firm hand she had reached out and covered the shape that was protruding from beneath the material. She had stroked the shape rhythmically, and Palmer had gasped with pleasure.

Finally she had released the shape from beneath the shorts and given it the same intimate attention that she had seen in the film earlier, the same intimate attention she had promised Palmer as she had whispered in his ear.

After a few minutes of this intimate contact she had turned back to face her man and had taken him. His excitement had been so great by that time that it was all over in a few minutes. It hadn't seemed to matter though and when they'd parted company later that night they'd arranged to meet again in the near future.

As he picked up the story he remembered that the future had arrived. He looked at his watch and checked the date. Palmer picked up the story he was telling at the point where it was sometime after one in the morning when he'd gone to leave.

Just as he'd got into his car, which he had left round the back in the car park that belonged to the flats, someone from an adjacent block had come out carrying what looked like a very heavy carpet. They dumped it in the boot of a dark red Jag and sped off up the road.

It had seemed odd to Palmer that someone would want to move a carpet that late at night. Also the way the Jag was driven made him suspicious, so he had decided to follow it. The car had careered through several streets and had made impact with at least three other vehicles. It looked quite badly damaged but the power of the Jag had eventually enabled the driver to lose Palmer. A couple of days later Karen had phoned him to say that a woman in the next block of flats had mysteriously disappeared and that the police suspected foul play. Palmer had immediately made a statement about the incident with the Jag and had then put it about his circle of friends to see if anything had turned up. That was a month ago, and so far no one had seen or heard of the car, or the woman for that matter.

"Well, that should do it." The mechanic appeared from the inspection pit. "Just refill it and bleed the tubes. So you think she might have been in the carpet?"

"Don't know, but it is possible. If they can find the car, then there might be some evidence in it."

"They won't find it. It'll either have gone abroad or it'll be in some lock up, or it may have been destroyed. If it hasn't been destroyed it will have been cleaned. And what about a body?"

"No, no body either. To date she's just someone who disappeared under mysterious circumstances."

"Like what?"

"Like her old man was away on business at the time. Out of the country. Actually my lady friend knows the couple and he called me in on this. I can prove he was nearly five hundred miles away when she disappeared. He had been for three days, and was for a further two days. He reported her missing when he got back and then a day or so later I got this call to see if I could help. That was after I told the cops about the car. Shame I couldn't keep up with it."

"Yeah, but you weren't ever gonna do that."

"No, not in this thing, but it's great for surveillance. It just blends in with the scenery, but it's useless for following cars at speed."

"Yeah. Anyway, I'll keep my eyes open for you. If I hear anything you'll be first to know."

"Thanks Pete, now how much for this?"

"Call it ten."

"Call it twenty." Palmer handed over the twenty-pound note he was proffering.

"Cheers Damien, now you take it easy, and don't forget I'm always available if you need assistance."

"Yeah, I haven't forgotten, and thanks for fixing this."

"That's no problem at all. Just take it easy for a bit and go carefully."

Palmer got into the car and started the engine. He backed the car out of the garage and waved his farewells as he backed into the road. He re-joined the one-way system and was soon heading for his appointment with Nash and their mutual client.

The mechanic had taken a little over half an hour to fix the car and it was now after four o'clock. The traffic was building up as the rush hour approached. Palmer drove slowly and carefully at first, testing the brakes at periodic intervals. He relaxed when he discovered they worked perfectly.

Palmer picked up his mobile phone and dialled a number.

"Karen, it's Damien. How are you?" A pause as the woman replied. "Yeah, that's great. Just ringing to check you're still on for this evening?" Another, shorter pause. "You are, great. I'll pick you up at, shall we say, eight." Another short pause followed. "Well, how about half past then?" Another pause. "Half eight it is. I've booked a table. Hope that's all right." A final, short, pause. "See you then. Bye darling." Palmer returned the mobile phone to the passenger seat and drove on to his appointment with Nash.

***

It was just before five o'clock when Palmer entered the offices of Goodland, Peasbody, and Nash. The receptionist was waiting for him and showed him directly to the office of John Nash.

"One moment Mr. Palmer," she said as she knocked on the door of Nash's office.

"Come", the voice inside was authoritative yet polite. The receptionist opened the door.

"Mr. Palmer has arrived sir."

"Thank-you. Please, show him in and then you may as well go home. It's almost time."

"Thank-you, Mr. Palmer, do please go in." As she spoke, the receptionist stood back and allowed Palmer to enter the room.

"Mr. Palmer thank you for coming." As Nash spoke, the receptionist discreetly closed the office door.

"Sorry I'm late, a spot of traffic trouble I'm afraid. Good evening Miss Cavendish."

Palmer had noted the woman sat in the interview chair and as she had not turned to acknowledge him he took the initiative.

"Good evening Mr. Palmer." Her voice was unsteady and Palmer noticed that she was wearing the same clothes she had worn to his home a few days ago. She turned to face the sleuth and smiled a watery, strained, smile.

"Mr. Palmer," Nash began, "to bring you up to date, Miss Cavendish has been released on bail and has to report to the police station every forty eight hours. We need to know how your investigations are progressing and then work out a plan of action. Meantime the police will doubtless be following their own lines of enquiry."

"Sure. Well, there hasn't been an enormous amount of progress yet but I am hopeful. I have uncovered a few matters but as yet I am afraid I can't provide you with the alibi you need, at least not one that would stand up in court." Palmer smiled to himself. It would, he considered, be easy to assume a few things and come up with a half-baked alibi. The only trouble would be the destruction of such a fabrication in court. It would do his credibility no good whatsoever, and his client would undoubtedly be imprisoned. Palmer decided that until the assumptions could be based in fact, he would not come up with a hypothesis for an alibi.

Palmer turned and faced the woman. He sat down on the chair that Nash provided and as he did so he positioned it so that he could look both at Nash and at Cavendish with relative ease. "But first, Miss Cavendish, if you don't mind I must ask you some questions."

"I'm feeling very tired Mr. Palmer. Can't it wait till tomorrow?"

"I'd prefer to ask them now. I have a busy night ahead and it really would help to hear your side of things first." Palmer's voice was reassuring, kind and mild.

"A busy night?" Her question was weary, if not a little strained. Palmer also detected a feint trace of intrigue and concern.

"Yes, I have two people to visit. One is at six-thirty, and the other later this evening. Now, do you mind if we start?"

"If I must, though I think I've already told you everything I can remember."

"Is it all right for you Mr. Nash if I question your client." Palmer deferred to the solicitor out of professional necessity rather than any friendship.

"Of course it is. But I suggest we keep it short. Miss Cavendish is very tired and needs to get home."

"Understood. In which case Miss Cavendish, I'd like to go back to the week of the crash. You said a few days ago that you went out for a meal with the Baker's on the night before they died. That would have been June 12th, is that correct?"

"Yes. I had spent the day with Sam. We'd done some girlie things, been shopping that sort of thing. Anyway, as they were going out in the evening they invited me to join them."

"Now this is very important. Was anyone else there with you?"

"Let me think now. Yes, that must have been the time. I think we went out with John's colleague from work. Might not have been then, but I think it was."

"Do you remember his name?"

"No." She paused as if thinking. Palmer watched her eyes closely though she was looking at Nash rather than himself. "No, sorry, I don't remember." Her eyes gave away the lie.

"Okay, it doesn't matter. It will only take me ten minutes to find out this evening. Now, do you remember which restaurant you went to?"

"Again, I'm sorry, but I can't remember. I know John and Sam loved Chinese food and I can remember it was that kind of a meal, but I can't remember the name."

"Or where the restaurant was?"

"Only vaguely, I'm hopeless at reading maps and that sort of thing. I drive purely from instinct. The Baker's lived in Sutton. You know that from the report. Well, I was staying with them and it was a short ride. Somewhere in Cheam, I think. Not the village, but further up the road. I've driven round the area since it all happened but I couldn't find it again. Maybe I got the direction wrong or something."

"Yeah. Easy thing to do in the dark, especially when you're not driving." Palmer had decided to play down the situation yet at the same time he had got the distinct impression that Cavendish was holding something back for some reason or other. "Now, you say you met up with this colleague of Mr. Baker. Did he come with you in the car, or did you meet him there?"

"Oh, met him there. Nice chap I seem to remember. You know, poor Sam, she was taken ill during the meal and he offered to drive her home. John, of course, wouldn't hear of it. So John and Sam left early and I sat there with this stranger." The woman paused and bit her lip as if she had said more than she ought to have done. She started to go even paler than before.

"Miss Cavendish, are you all right?" Nash intervened.

"Yes, I'm fine. I've just remembered something that's all. Silly really. His name's Richard, I think. Now don't get me wrong, I'm not that kind of woman really. I'm not the sort that just sits in restaurants with strangers."

"Sorry Miss Cavendish, you've lost me." Palmer was still sitting back in his chair, quite relaxed.

"Well, I remember now. Sam was ill so John and she went home early. That left Richard and me. Of course I'd never met Richard before but it was clear that we were ending up as partners for the evening. Anyway when the Bakers went home it just left the two of us.

John had talked to Richard as they were leaving. Don't know what he'd said but after the

Baker's left Richard offered me a lift back. I wasn't really thinking straight before. He offered me a lift back because I'd come with the Baker's and otherwise I would've had to get a cab back." Her voice sounded agitated and tired, yet Palmer felt convinced that Cavendish knew far more than she was letting on.

"So Richard took you back to the Baker's later that evening?"

"No. He suggested we went on to a club he knew. Well, by the end of the meal I'd got to know him a bit better and I was feeling like doing something so I agreed. From what I remember the club was dead boring and we left about eleven or so I guess. Then he took me back to my place. It seemed okay at the time, but I'd had quite a lot to drink. It was only when we pulled up at my flat that I remembered Sam had suggested I stayed over. I'd protested because I hadn't got anything to wear and she'd said that didn't matter. In any case she'd picked me up in the morning and we'd done some shopping, and she wouldn't have wanted to drive me back late at night.

Anyhow, when we got up to the flat it was late. I invited Richard up for coffee. He'd been the perfect gentleman up until then and coffee was the least I could give him when he'd driven me back to Wimbledon.

When we got inside he said I should just phone them and let them know I was okay. I guess if Sam was ill she wouldn't have wanted me around anyway. I rang the Baker's but the answer phone was on so I left them a message telling them I'd gone home with Richard. He had coffee and left. I went to bed and that was that."

"And the following day?" Palmer prompted her gently.

"I can't remember much, apart from waking up to a knock on the door early in the morning. I'm sorry," she started to sob, "but the shock of what happened has completely made me forget. I'm sorry."

"Hmm." Palmer sat in the chair with his two index fingers poised under his lower lips and his hands clasped together. "That ties in with the reports and your statements. But there is something not quite right. Maybe something you have forgotten, or something that you have remembered erroneously."

"I don't know. It's what I remember Mr. Palmer. Of course it may not be quite right. It was sixteen months ago."

"Yes of course. Now you are tired and no doubt need to get home. I would offer you a lift myself but I am in rather a rush this evening. Can we get you a cab?" Palmer stole a glance at Nash, a glance that said, "I need to talk to you alone".

"Thank you, a taxi would be fine. Oh, did you find what you were looking for in my flat the other evening?" She asked the sleuth.

"Well, I didn't know what I was looking for in the first place and no I didn't find anything that would help with this matter. Didn't really expect to after all this time. But it was worth the try."

"Oh I see."

"Well, it was a long shot really. But this time I guess the shot was just that bit too far."

"Oh well, thank you for trying."

"Oh, and the keys have been destroyed."

"Thank you."

Nash phoned the local taxi company and in a few minutes the woman was on her way home.

"You wanted to talk?" Nash started as soon as the taxi had left.

"Yes. I wondered what you thought of that little performance back there?"

"Performance? I thought she did pretty well in the circumstances."

"You didn't spot anything unusual?"

"No, did you?"

"Well, let's just say that if she was telling the whole truth then I'm a monkey's uncle. I can't quite put my finger on it yet, but I just know she's not telling us everything."

"You're wrong, Palmer. She's just tired and frightened. Who wouldn't be after what she's going through."

"Tired I will grant you, but she is not frightened. The psychology of the woman was wrong. No, you will soon find that she was playing a very clever game with us. In fact, you may well find that she started playing the little game the moment she contacted Goodland. There is something altogether wrong with the frightened Miss Cavendish. Something about her is most definitely not frightened, mark my words."

"If you say so but look, it's getting late. Can we talk again, maybe tomorrow?"

"Assuredly. I'll ring you in the morning. Might have some more news by then. Must go anyway, I have another appointment to keep. Goodnight."

"Until tomorrow then, and you are wrong about Miss Cavendish."

"Until tomorrow, we shall see."

Chapter 6

Palmer walked away from the solicitors and found his car. He sat in the car for some minutes without moving, but all the time he was thinking hard. He turned the ignition key until the radio sprang to life. Almost without thinking, and without seeming to care as to its content, he pushed the cassette back into the drive bay. After a few seconds the rhythmic strains of Eric Clapton filled the car. Palmer sat back and placed his hands behind his head, as the music continued. He sat this way for several minutes, pondering the different angels of the Cavendish case.

His mind drifted back to a previous case. It had been an awkward case and he'd received help from an unexpected source, a source that had made him think, and think hard. Karen Shaw had been acquainted with Palmer for over a year though their relationship had only really become relatively stable over the past couple of months or so. She was into computers in as much as she made her life from designing software for some big company. Her passion though lay in a completely different direction. The product of strict Christian parents, she had rebelled at the age of eighteen when she'd gone to university to study for her computing degree. Turning away from her religion she looked beyond the narrow sheltered life of her past and began to explore other options. It was not long before she found she had certain skills that could not be entirely attributed to the natural.

Once at university she began to dabble with the occult and it was during this time that she first started getting the pictures, as she called them. Though they started almost as a flash of a scene that disappeared almost as soon as it had started, these flashes soon developed into what were sometimes several seconds of moving actions. She found that the more she explored the occult the more often and more intense the images became. Although her friends ridiculed her to start with they treated her more seriously when, after a clear picture of a motorbike being crushed by a huge juggernaut, she failed to stop her boyfriend at the time going home the following weekend.

Her friends shared her horror and grief when early on the Saturday morning they learned that he'd been involved in a crash on the motorway. Apparently, on the Friday night, he'd skidded on a particularly wet piece of road and lost control. His bike had swerved from the central lane to the nearside lane and had ended up being crushed by the juggernaut that he'd just overtaken.

The tragedy left a severe impression on the young girl and she vowed not to play with the cards or board again. Indeed she had removed every last item of regalia that could be linked to the occult, but for some reason the visions continued. It was as if she had unlocked a link to the supernatural, a link that would not be severed.

After university she had once again tried to get involved in the church, but to no avail. Her visions continued and when she chose to tell others about them she was ostracised and rejected. Gradually over a few years her visions subsided until once again they reverted to almost flashes of insight. This troubled her less as they were more or less now just ideas, thoughts, guesses, with none of the horror of the full graphic images she had previously experienced.

Then she had met Palmer. She had been the lecturer on a computer course and he had been one of the pupils, despite being a good few years older than she. She had been fascinated that a Private Investigator should want to learn all about the Internet and had spent some time conversing with him during the lunch interval on the first day. She found his work fascinating, and at the same time he showed genuine interest in her work. There was something about him that intrigued her and so, at the end of the three-day course when he had asked her out for dinner, she had been only too willing to agree.

Palmer recalled that their first date had been amicable if not particularly romantic. She was a fiercely independent woman, and at the time the three days had greatly interfered with a case he was working on. It could have been a straightforward case of search and find but it had proved up to that point to be more difficult than expected. During the course of their meal, Karen had, perhaps foolishly, asked him to tell her about some of the cases he'd worked on.

Maintaining the anonymity of his client he'd gone on to explain that a particular woman had become involved in betting on the greyhounds over the phone. There was this syndicate that had good insider knowledge but as a result could not lay bets easily. Over a few months she'd laid bets and won a reasonable amount of money. Then, as with all scams, the ante had gone up, to over a £1000. It was more than she could afford but the history was good. Again, as always, she was told to lay the bet at a specific betting office by phone and in a name she'd used previously. Always before she'd got her share of the winnings within a few days, always cash, and always by post. Without realising what was happening that is what she did. Needless to say the greyhound won, at seven to one.

The days passed and she heard nothing. No winnings arrived. A week passed and there were still no winnings. After two weeks she tried the telephone number she'd been given. Perhaps not surprisingly the number was discontinued. At that point she had contacted Palmer and told him everything. There was little enough to go on. An envelope and a copy of the last cheque she had received, and it had not been enough. The letter had been posted from Birmingham whilst the cheque was from an account in Somerset. Palmer had quickly realised that there was virtually no chance in solving the case and finding the perpetrator of the fraud.

Then, at that point in his description of the case, Karen had frozen for a moment. Palmer had been looking at her and noticed the momentary change in her countenance.

"What's the matter?" He asked the woman.

"Nothing. It's just that I occasionally get these sort of images in my mind."

"Oh. What was it?" Palmer sounded somewhat sceptical though the woman was used to such a reaction and was unperturbed by it.

"Well. I saw a racecourse. Horse racing. There was a big white building, with a great glass front, and a roundabout. In front of the building there was a short man in a brown coat and tweed cap. He was talking on a mobile phone. His pockets looked like they were stuffed with cash. That's all."

"That's quite a picture." Palmer had feigned interest. After all, he reasoned, he was talking about greyhound racing and not horse racing, so it just proved his scepticism was justified. The rest of the evening had passed amicably enough and they had agreed to swap phone numbers and stay in touch.

Less than a week later Palmer had been driving along Epsom Downs past the racecourse. As he approached the roundabout by the grandstand he almost crashed when he saw the brown-coated man in a tweed cap standing in front of the building. In his hand was a mobile phone and his pockets were bulging. Palmer drove twice round the roundabout and took a better look at the man. A few days later the national papers had been full of the story of the great racing swindler who'd set up a network of syndicates each playing against each other and all the time pouring money into his pockets. The swindler though, was known by none of the syndicate's members as all contact was over a mobile phone, and the paper was appealing for help in tracing the man. Within minutes of reading the article Palmer was talking to the police. A few days later the man had been arrested and charged and Palmer had had to think back to Karen's image that first evening they'd been together.

As he remembered that case, the strains of "Wonderful Tonight" drifted through the car. As

131

they did so Palmer came slowly out of his reverie, looking forward to his own wonderful night. First though, it was time for some more work.

His next appointment was crucial and he needed to make a few adjustments to his appearance beforehand. Hastily he removed the suit jacket and the tie and replaced it with a sweater. He found the pair of dark-rimmed spectacles he always carried in the car. They were blanks, or in other words the lenses were not powered, but the spectacles were effective as part of a disguise. Next Palmer rummaged around in the bottom of his briefcase and finally withdrew an identity card. He placed the card and the mobile phone carefully on the passenger seat, together with a reporter's notebook and a couple of ball-pens. Finally he started the car. He was not in a hurry, which was a good thing. The traffic, he soon discovered, was heavier than he had expected. It soon became clear that the roads were becoming clogged with the additional load of the rush hour. He joined the queues and made his way to the appointment.

It was just before six thirty when Palmer reached his destination. He'd had to check out the final part of the route, and the road itself, using an ordnance survey map. It was unfamiliar territory to him and he drove past "The Laurels" almost before he had spotted the name plaque in the dark. The plaque itself was made in the shape of a log with the lettering burnt into the wood. Palmer played with the poetic notion that it might even have been a log from a laurel tree.

He drove past the house a reasonable distance and then turned round. Retracing his steps he easily found the driveway. The house, Palmer noted, was large and detached, and boasted a through drive. The driveway itself was shingled and Palmer pulled up outside the front door. To the side of the house was a double garage and in front of the garage was parked a dark blue one year old four wheel drive off road vehicle which, Palmer considered, was probably close to the top of the range for that particular make of vehicle. Even in the dark it oozed quality.

He noted down the index number of the vehicle in the back of his notebook and then, having looked quickly round the rest of the driveway, he walked briskly to the front door and pressed the bell button. Inside, and incongruous to this kind of residence, a catchy tune started to play. As it did so he heard the menacing growl of what sounded like a fairly large dog. The growl became a much louder and fiercer bark as the door was opened.

"Yes? Who is it?" The male voice from within was obviously struggling with the canine brute that was still invisible to Palmer.

"John Adams. I called you earlier."

"Oh yeah. Hang on a tick while I lock the dog up."

"Sure. No problems." Palmer's voice sounded relieved that he would not have to encounter the animal. The door was barely open and Palmer could see little of what lay within. He stood patiently on the doorstep, listening to the struggle that was taking place within.

"Maisie, come on girl, in here," he heard the voice cajoling the animal into a distant room.

Moments later he heard a door shut, followed by the sound of footsteps returning.

"I'm sorry about that. She's harmless really, but does tend to get a bit over-excited when there are strangers around."

"Oh. What breed is she?"

"Doberman. She's a wonderful dog, well bitch actually in this case. Do come in." The owner of the dog opened the door fully and Palmer extended his hand in greeting.

"Mr. Derwent, nice to meet you, and thanks for seeing me at such short notice."

"That's not a problem, Mr. Adams. Reporter you say. Who do you work for?"

"Oh, here and there, I'm freelance. It gives me opportunities to do interesting articles like the one I talked to you about."

"Yes. Poor John, that is my ex-partner, now very sadly deceased." Palmer could almost guarantee the voice was feigning mourning. "Mysterious accidents that went unresolved, that was the title wasn't it? Tea, coffee, something stronger?"

"Well, if you have it I'm partial to a scotch on the rocks. Otherwise coffee will be fine. Yes, something along those lines. It's still very much what we call a working title. It'll probably end up being called something altogether much shorter and snappier."

"So, how do I fit in?"

"Well, one of my researchers picked up on the Baker case, as we call it, and did a bit of digging. Seemed like it was just an accident that had no reason, and as that's essentially what the article will be about I got landed with doing some work on it too. Of course it didn't take long to track down Mr. Baker's origins and his business activities etc. All of that kind of stuff is, of course, really boring for the reader. Then, as you might suspect, out of the proverbial woodwork came his business partner. So I thought I'd see if you could maybe put a different angle on things – try and make my article a bit more interesting."

"Well, I could try. Where do you want me to start? Here, scotch on the rocks. Hope it's okay."

Palmer took a tentative sip. "Excellent. Must be a Glenfiddich I should say."

"That's remarkable, you're spot on. Bet you can't tell me which year though?"

"Not the last three, that's for sure. Other than that I'm not such an expert."

"Nineteen seventy six." Derwent sounded triumphant.

"Seventy-six eh. That's great. Tell you what, why don't we start with the victims? Tell me what you know about them. You don't mind if I make notes, do you?"

"Notes? You don't use a recorder?"

"No. I prefer my shorthand. It keeps everything private and I can just write down the interesting bits and pieces – helps to pull the article together later on.

"Right, I see." Derwent didn't sound convinced, but he carried on anyway. "John Baker and I met shortly after University. I was working for some firm or other up in London and not doing very well. John was also working up there for a different company. Anyhow, as I recall we met at some convention and found that firstly we lived a stone's throw from each other – we had flats in town at the time, secondly we were in the same line of business, and thirdly we both shared an interest in rugby. So we kept in touch for some months and went to a few games together. Then John met Samantha at some works do or other I think. They went out with each other for about a year before they got engaged. I went to the wedding and then shortly after that they moved out to Sutton. They found a nice little house and John set up in business on his own. Well, his business took off and he was soon looking round for help. I guess I bought into the idea and so Baker and Derwent was formed. After a bit I moved here. This place is much more convenient for the office.

Anyway John and I were pretty close. We shared a lot of time out of the office, watching rugger, drinking, and those kinds of things. I got to know Sam quite well, but she wasn't really into sport or drinking so she tended not to come with John on our little jaunts. But, she was a damned good hostess."

"I see, so they were just an ordinary couple really."

"Yes, that's how I'd describe them, an ordinary couple. John did once tell me something about his wife but it's not really relevant to your article."

"Go on, you never know."

"Well, he found out about it a few months after they'd got married. Apparently she'd been to University, but not the same as him, and I don't know which one. While she was there she'd had this fling with some trainee law student. Apparently

136

it all got very passionate. Anyway she went along to one of their dos at the end of a term. According to John, she got into a situation that ended up with her being taken by a gang of them. There were five of them and when they noticed she was getting drunk they bundled her into a van and drove it round the town while they took turns with her – all against her will, you understand. Well, that incident nearly put her off men for life, but John was different. He was kind and compassionate. He lulled her and wooed her and never asked her what it was all about, but she told him anyway after they were married. Well, the story went that she vowed to get even with the men that had taken advantage of her. Apparently two of them had already met with their demise. Not physically, you understand, but their careers had been ruined. According to John, just before the accident she'd located the third guy. It had taken a few years but she was determined to get even. She was going to expose him or something, probably as she did with the other ones. Anyway there was definitely some scandal about to come out of it all."

"And you told the police all this?"

"Nah. It was all speculation, no proof. John almost treated her intentions and claims as a joke – she was obviously disturbed by the gang bang and it was her way of getting it out of her system."

"Yeah, but over what, ten years?"

"I suppose, when you say it like that, that it is a long time. Anyway, if you knew Sam, she couldn't have organised a trip to the coast, let alone plot to bring down a solicitor." Derwent laughed a small, polite, laugh.

"Maybe. Anyway, we can probably work something out of it, discreetly of course. Would have made a nice angle though."

"What would've done?"

"Oh something like, solicitor afraid of being exposed arranges death of woman he raped ten years ago."

"Hey, that's not bad. But it didn't happen like that. Another drink?"

"Oh, thanks." Palmer waited while his glass was refreshed. "So, how did it happen?"

"It was all quite simple really. I'd just pulled off a big business deal. Well it was big for John and myself. So I suggested we went out for a meal. Well, John's married but I'm single and at the time I didn't have a steady partner. However, his wife suggested she brought along this other woman and I agreed. I presumed she was a friend from Sam's own circle of friends. Anyway we met up at the restaurant and had the starters. Then Sam got feverish and I think she was sick. Anyhow, upshot of it was John had to take her home. So I got left on my own with this other woman. Had a very pleasant evening and I ended up taking her home. Might add I ended up going in for coffee, if you know what I mean."

"And that was the night of the accident?"

"Sure. Didn't know it then, but they ran right off the road on the way home. Nothing suspicious about it either, just a plain old accident. Of course, we didn't hear about it until the next morning."

"You mean, when you were at work?"

"Lord no. I was still round at the woman's. The police reckoned she was Samantha's nearest relative, a cousin, or something. Police wanted her to identify the body. Right state she got into. Anyway we went along. I identified John and she identified Samantha. Didn't see much of her after that. I think she went away for a bit, once the funerals were over that is."

"Oh. Let me check this back. The four of you met up at a restaurant."

"Yeah."

"You can't remember its name can you – only some of the readers are into the details?"

"Sure. It's my favourite. The Peeking Duck."

"Oh right, I seem to know that name. That's pretty famous isn't it?"

"Well, I suppose you could say that. You know it?"

"I don't think I've been there, but I've seen it advertised somewhere."

"You were saying before that?"

"Sorry. You met up at the Peeking Duck, and started your meal. Your partner's wife gets ill and they leave. Somewhere on the way home they crash and get killed. You spent the night with a woman who turned out to be a cousin and next morning you both found out about the accident?"

"That's about it. Not much of a story is it?"

"No. Just that when my researcher pulled a few articles on it, it looked promising. Guess there isn't much of a story in it after all. No scandal, no illicit affairs, no drugs, nothing like that?" The question was meant to be rhetorical but Derwent chose to answer it.

"Well, no drugs that's for sure. The police did all the usual tests and nothing untoward was found.

As for scandal, that doesn't seem likely. I'd known them for years and they were just the kind of people to keep themselves to themselves."

"And there were no illicit affairs either?" Palmer smiled inoffensively.

"Good Lord, no." His answer was, Palmer thought, just a little bit too quick and just a tiny bit too forceful. "Not unless there was any truth in her ridiculous story about getting even with a bunch of solicitors. But that was just her way of coping, a kind of fantasy. So no, there were no illicit affairs."

"Hmm. Well, it all seems a bit of a non-event really, a definitely sad event, but non-event. Anyway I'm very grateful for your time, and I am sorry it has ended up being wasted. Still, you will receive a token of thanks in due course."

"Is that the end of it all now then?"

"Oh, I should think so, unless the damned researchers turn up anything new. Not very likely in this case I should say. Sad thing is I've got to do another one of these chats tomorrow evening, and that case looks far less interesting than this one did an hour ago. Anyway I've taken up enough of your time so I had better go and leave you in peace."

"Sorry I couldn't help you more than I did. Anyway thanks for the chat, and if you do turn up anything you will let me know won't you?"

"Of course."

Palmer was now standing just outside the front door. He turned and climbed into his car. As he did so, he switched off the tape recorder in his pocket.

The engine started first time and in a moment he was indicating to turn right out of the drive. As he turned out of the drive the front door behind him was closed. The country road was a long one and there were few turnings. Palmer had driven perhaps half a mile when he met a small, light coloured car coming in the other direction. He thought the car was travelling rather fast as it approached and its speed meant he only got a quick glance at the driver. It was enough to tell him that it was a female. She had short, fair hair with a fringe on the front. She was wearing glasses and some kind of red blouse or jumper. Palmer couldn't be sure. But he was sure the face looked even familiar, even with the split second glance that he had snatched. In an instant the car was behind him, its taillights rapidly disappearing in his rear view mirror.

As the light coloured car continued on its journey something at the back of Palmer's mind caused him to react. In an instant he had braked sharply and started the process of turning the car round. As a practised hand at car pursuits it took Palmer only a few seconds before he was pointing in the same direction as the light coloured car. Indeed, he could still see the taillights of the car in the distance. For several seconds Palmer seemed to be gaining on the car, then quite suddenly and without indicating the car pulled off into a drive.

Palmer judged the distance and nodded knowingly to himself. He slowed his own car until his speed was respectable. Deliberately he drove past the drive into which the light coloured car had turned. As he did so, he noticed the female occupant alighting from her vehicle. Again Palmer nodded to himself. He drove for perhaps a further hundred metres at which distance there was a gateway to a field. Palmer pulled in and turned off the engine.

There was no time for preparation or disguise. In a moment he was out of the car and running back up the road to the driveway.

By the time he arrived, slightly breathless from the exertion, the woman had evidently gone into the house, the same house that Palmer had left only a few minutes beforehand. Before approaching the house Palmer bent down and passed behind the passenger side of the light coloured car. He had already noted the index number of the car. It was familiar to him. Now he peered in through the window. His hooded torchlight picked out the mobile phone tossed carelessly on the passenger seat. He continued the examination carefully but saw little else of interest.

In a moment his attention was turned to the house. He noticed for the second time that evening the double-glazing on the windows. In the lounge the curtains were drawn, but badly, and a clear shaft of light was shining onto the driveway. Palmer inched himself under the window and with infinite care peered in through the window.

He could see enough of what was happening though the actions were animated and he could hear nothing. On the large settee the woman, less her glasses, was gesticulating at the man. Palmer judged that the woman was not best pleased with Richard Derwent. Indeed, why the woman was there at all was more than a passing curiosity to the sleuth. Palmer watched her antics for several minutes. It seemed from her actions that she was extremely angry. From the man's own actions Palmer could surmise that Derwent was being extremely apologetic and on a number of occasions he reached out a conciliatory hand for it to be slapped away by the woman.

Palmer was musing to himself that this was the same woman who, only a few hours earlier had seemed pale, withdrawn and frightened. Now though, something had clearly changed all that. She was a woman scorned, or at best deeply hurt. Palmer was still trying to work out exactly what Helen Cavendish was doing in the home of Richard Derwent when the scene changed dramatically. In an instant that almost dazed the detective, Cavendish stood up, took a well-aimed swipe at the subject of her anger and stormed out of the room. Palmer almost reacted too slowly. Indeed, he had only just found relative cover behind a large rhododendron bush when the front door of the house was thrown open.

"Don't you fucking well come near me again, you bastard. You swore it was a once off but it wasn't." The woman was obviously continuing her tirade of abuse even as she opened her own car door. She started the engine and wound down the window. As she screeched away from the house she vented her anger once more.

"And if either you, or that fucking whore come near me again, or make up any other lies about me, I'll do you both."

Palmer was shocked. This was quite a different Cavendish to the one who had knocked on his door a few days ago, and quite a different Cavendish to the one who had sat pale and frightened in her solicitor's office just a few hours ago. Palmer saw Derwent standing at the front of the door. In the porch light Palmer could see the swelling of the bruise starting to form under his right eye. It looked painful. In a moment the door was shut and Palmer was relieved to be able to straighten up.

He made the hundred metres back to his car in under a minute. He wasn't rushing. There was no point in trying to catch up with the car. He knew where she'd be going and in any event he had other things to sort out that evening. Palmer reached his car and started the engine. Soon he was driving back down the country road, his mind trying to unravel the evening's events.

Palmer continued driving and arrived home a little after seven thirty. He had an hour to prepare for the evening. It had been nearly a month since he'd seen Karen and he was looking forward to their evening together.

Chapter 7

It was exactly eight thirty when Palmer knocked on the door of the young woman's apartment. Sutton was becoming an all too frequent name in Palmer's itinerary over the past few days but this evening he felt relaxed. He'd found the restaurant in the Yellow Pages shortly after he'd got home and was lucky to find they had a table free at nine thirty. So he'd decided to break one of his golden rules and to mix a little business with some pleasure. How much business would be involved he didn't know and he certainly wasn't about to let on that the evening was partly business related.

The door opened slowly and Karen stood there. She was only just thirty years old, a stunning five feet nine inches or so Palmer reckoned. Her sandy coloured hair flowed down her back past her shoulder blades. In the light of her doorway Palmer thought her face looked particularly attractive. Her radiant smile set off the black silky, thigh length dress she was wearing. That together with her calf length boots made her look particularly attractive.

"Punctual as ever," she laughed as the door opened.

"Of course, and you look really great. Good job we're going somewhere nice."

"Wouldn't matter if we weren't. How are you Damien?" She reached over and kissed him tenderly on his cheek as he entered the hallway.

"I'm not at all bad. Keeping busy and all that. How are you?"

"Hmm. Not so bad I suppose."

"Problems?"

"No. Just one of those days at the office."

"Busy?"

"Yeah. Didn't even get a lunch break. And to add to it all, the boss was being a right sod this afternoon. Reckon he went to the pub at lunchtime. Something's not right with him anyway."

"Oh, one of those days was it? Yeah, I guess mine's been a bit like that too."

"Oh, come on Damien. You work for yourself. How can it be like that?"

"Quite easily actually. I may be my own boss, but I still can't choose my clients you know. Anyway we agreed not to mix business with pleasure didn't we?"

"Yeah, that's true. What time are we eating?"

"Nine-thirty. And it's only about ten minutes from here. So if we leave at nine we should be there in plenty of time. You do like Cantonese don't you."

"Yeah. I like all that Oriental stuff. You ever tried Jap. Food?"

"No, can't say I have."

"Well, you wait until you do. It's very different. Do you fancy a drink first then?"

As she spoke, the woman started to walk back to the living room. Palmer dutifully followed.

"Please. Scotch if you have it."

"With ice, but no water isn't it. See, I did remember, and you know what that means."

"Yes, ice no water, and maybe, later."

The woman leaned over the cabinet where she stored the drinks bottles and Palmer noticed from her curves that she was not wearing any support. Her full breasts became partly visible under the strong light that was hidden under a ledge of the cabinet, and with it Palmer could see the contours of her nipples. He smiled to himself appreciatively but the smile had vanished before she turned towards him with the drink.

"Scotch, ice and no water."

Palmer took a seat on the sofa and allowed her to hand him the drink. He took the offered glass and as he did so she seductively dragged her fingers over the fist that now held the glass. Her touch was warm and gentle and Palmer shuddered slightly.

"Do you like what I'm wearing, or is it a bit too daring." She stood up now and pushed her breasts out in front of her as far as they would go, showing off her womanly features to the enraptured Palmer.

"You look great, as always. And no, it's not too daring. Actually you could wear it off the shoulders a bit if you really wanted. You've got such a good figure it would work well like that."

"Flatterer. What, like this?" With that she pulled the dress straps down over her shoulders so that the whole dress was lowered by a couple of inches. The effect of this was to show off even more of her cleavage and it clearly pleased the detective as he sat there smiling pleasantly.

"Come on, we'd better stop playing games, or we'll never get to the restaurant."

"I don't mind if you don't." The woman was now admiring her chest, though admiring it in a teasing sort of way.

"You're not hungry?"

"Yes, but food isn't everything."

147

"Maybe not, but it's damned important if you haven't eaten since breakfast. Look, can we pick this up a bit later?"

"Spoilsport," she said as she plopped down on the sofa next to the man. "Well, at least give me a kiss then."

Palmer obliged. He placed the glass on the nearby table and embraced the woman. They kissed tenderly to start with but in a moment became more passionate as first their lips and then tongues found each other. They remained like this for several minutes, exploring each other's mouths. After about five minutes Palmer broke off the contact.

"Come on babe, we'd better go, or we'll miss the table."

"Hmm, okay then. Just one more little kiss first."

"Oh, all right then." Palmer smiled and once again their tongues embraced in a detailed oral examination.

It was some minutes later when they finally left the flat and walked down the stairway to Palmer's car that was parked at the rear of the block of flats. The drive to the restaurant took only a few minutes and by half past nine they were sitting at the table that had been reserved for them.

"So, Damien, how did you get to hear about this place?" The woman asked him just as the waiter left the table having taken the order.

"Oh, I saw it advertised somewhere. Something like it's got a Michelin award or something. Anyway I thought it's be different to our usual haunts."

"Yeah, and a good bit more pricey too."

"My treat so you don't have to worry about it."

"Your treat! You must be feeling guilty about something." She smiled sweetly and as she did so she reached under the table and laid her right hand on his left knee.

"Me, guilty?" He responded by placing a hand over hers.

"Yes, guilty. You only ever treat me when you've been up to something."

"Is that a fact. Well, where do you want me to start?"

"The beginning, as always."

"Okay. I'm on this case at the moment and this place came up in the investigations. So if I'm guilty of anything then it's mixing pleasure with just a tad of business."

"That's not it, Palmer. There's something else. You wouldn't treat me just for that."

"No?" His voice sounded intentionally hurt.

"No, and you know it."

"Oh well, I guess you'd better know the truth. I met this woman with really nice long brown hair and we ended up sleeping together." His voice sounded almost comical, like the little boy who got caught.

"Oh, that's all right then, I thought it was something serious."

"No, just a casual relationship." Palmer laughed, and his companion joined in too. As he laughed he wondered just what had happened to the casual relationship. He made a mental note to check it out the following day.

"You know we both have our own lives. It's just nice to be together sometimes. What you do in

149

between times, and what I do, for that matter, is entirely your own affair."

"Okay, so if it's my affair, you'd better tell me what you've been doing."

"You know what I mean, silly."

"Yeah, just playing on your grammar."

"And you know she's been dead for years, so leave her alone."

"Dead?" Palmer sounded confused, but then saw the joke and laughed. When his laughter had subsided he continued. "Are we going to spend all evening in this frame of mind?"

"Hope not, I've got other plans for you." She squeezed his leg affectionately and Palmer felt a stirring feeling under the tablecloth.

"Oops, hold on, here comes the starters."

The food was excellent and the good-natured banter continued as they ate. After nearly an hour they were still smiling, staring at each other over coffee.

"Great meal," the woman began. "Must come here again."

"Yeah. And it's all so clean. You could almost eat off the floor it's so shiny."

"Hmm, well I'll stick to plates thank you."

"Yeah, you're probably wise. Say, waiter, could we have the bill please?"

"Certainly sir." The accent was only just detectable as being oriental in its nature.

"Well," Palmer continued, "do you have to get up early tomorrow?"

"Fairly, why?" Karen replied.

"Just wondered what you had in mind for the rest of the evening."

"Well now, it's been about a month so I was hoping you might drive me home and then come in for coffee."

"But we've just had coffee."

"Okay so we skip the coffee. Does that suit sir?" There was a definite twinkle in her eye and she pushed out her breasts suggestively, not that Palmer needed any encouragement.

"Yes. That's fine. But I do have to get up early, so we can't be too late."

"Who said anything about staying up late. An early night would suit me fine." Her voice was suggestive and the added silky tones were a deliberate lure for her partner of the evening.

"Oh good, here comes the bill."

Palmer paid the waiter in cash and added a generous tip for which he received due thanks. As the couple rose to leave the same waiter fussed around them, almost unnecessarily, but evidently wanting to show his gratitude for their generosity. Finally, and with much ushering and goodnights having been spoken, Palmer and the woman returned to his car.

"Did you find out what you wanted to know?" Karen asked him as they pulled out of the car park.

"I think so, more or less. I'll contact the manager tomorrow just to check, but I'm pretty certain he won't be able to help."

"So what was it you wanted to know? I mean you stayed with me the whole evening, and I can't remember you asking anyone any particular question?" She sounded intrigued, as if he might have extracted some information using coded language.

151

"I wanted to know if someone dined here on a particular evening sixteen months ago."

"And you found that out? Boy that's clever from what I saw."

"Nope, but I did discover they probably couldn't tell me."

"How come?"

"Simple really, their booking lists are on photocopied pieces of paper and not in a diary. You only have to guess that they keep those sheets just long enough to reconcile the takings, and if you're lucky for a few more weeks for health reasons."

"But what about credit card slips or the till roll?"

"It's possible, but I've met the guy, and if he is up to what I think he is then he would almost certainly have paid in cash. So it's untraceable."

"What do you think he's up to?"

"Murder, probably, but proving it could take a while. At the moment it's little better than just a hunch, but there are a few things that don't quite fit in with each other, so something's amiss."

"Murder. That's a pretty big step from having a meal in a restaurant. Care to explain?"

"Can't really. It's just a hunch. Trouble is it seems likely, but I can't get the evidence together to make it a reality. And, to boot, it's all several months since the kind of evidence I need has almost certainly been destroyed."

"Oh."

"Yeah. One thing though, do you keep a diary?"

"Yes, I fill in stuff almost every day."

"Okay, well try this for size. Do you have your own name and telephone number in the address section?"

"No. What'd be the point? I don't even fill in the details on the personal section either."

"Exactly, who does? Except of course someone with a memory problem."

"Even then they surely wouldn't put their own details in the address section."

"That's what I thought. Left here, isn't it?" Palmer gesticulated at the signpost that the headlights of the car had just depicted.

"Oh, sorry, yes. Then second right, over the junction and it's on the left." At that precise moment Karen Shaw went very quiet, as if she had entered a sudden, and involuntary trance. It lasted only a few seconds and went unnoticed by Palmer.

"Thanks. And you're sure you want me to come upstairs when we get back?"

"Most definitely I want you to come upstairs, and I will be disappointed if you don't.

After all, it's my turn tonight isn't it? Anyway, look. I have a feeling. This case you're working on. The restaurant, somehow, it's a switch."

Palmer paused for a moment as if he was having difficulty recalling what her question meant. Having recalled their last encounter, he responded.

"Yes, it's your turn, assuming you're up for it. What do you mean a switch?"

"I don't know. It's just a feeling that somewhere in that restaurant, sixteen months ago, a switch was made. Nothing more than that for now, but I'll work on it if you want?"

This was one of the fascinating things that Palmer liked about the woman sitting next to him. It was as if, on certain occasions, she could dip into the past on a different plane, almost a supernatural plane, not that Palmer believed in such things. Yet it was fascinating.

"Yes, work on it. It might help. Anyway," he continued, "are you up for it?"

"You know I am. Haven't you taken any notice of my attentions this evening?"

"Yes, you know I have. It's just that I'm a bit preoccupied that's all."

"Well, you've got about two hundred yards to get un-preoccupied."

"Okay. No sooner said than done. There, totally un-preoccupied."

The couple parked the car where Palmer had left it earlier that evening and went indoors.

"Drink?" She asked as soon as they had taken off their coats.

"Okay, and while you're making it I'll go and get things ready."

"Hmm, sounds fun."

"It will be. Scotch, neat please."

With that Palmer left Karen in the sitting room and paid a brief visit to the bathroom and then the bedroom. On returning to the lounge he discovered the drink sitting patiently on the coffee table for him, and the soothing strains of a Mozart Concerto whispered softly from the darkened corners of the room.

Palmer sat in one of the armchairs and sipped the Scotch. "Hmm, that's nice. What are you drinking?"

154

"Rum and coke," she replied as she came and sat down on his lap. He put his arm round her, holding her gently. His hand started off round her waist, but after a few seconds he began to move it upwards until he felt the bottom of her breast. He continued more slowly until he could feel the nipple under his hand. He stroked her gently as she sat on his lap. He stroked her gently until he felt her legs open slightly and she squirmed with the pleasure he was giving her.

He carried on this way until the drinks were finished. By now she was breathing slightly heavily and had draped an arm around his neck. She took his glass and placed it on the table before turning on his lap and wrapping both arms tightly round his neck. She leaned forward until her lips touched his and they joined in a passionate embrace.

"Take me," she said quite simply as soon as their lips parted. Palmer rose, picking her up as he did so. Holding her in his arms he carried her into the bedroom. He laid her gently on the bed and unfastened her dress. He removed it with the deft skill of an experienced lover. She lay there on the bed with her eyes closed, wearing nothing but her black lace knickers, stockings and a suspender belt.

Palmer slowly unclasped each stocking. Then with infinite care he removed each stocking, in turn stroking her legs as he did so. Finally he slid the belt off her. The discarded garments lay in a pile beside the bed. Having removed the stockings he rolled her over so that she lay on her stomach. He reached out and picked up the little bottle of scented oil and then sitting astride her he gently, lovingly, massaged a little of the oil into her neck and back.

155

His practised hands moved slowly down her back, always gently massaging, always gently caressing. He reached the bikini line and stopped before devoting his attention to each leg in turn. Starting with the feet, he gently massaged a little of the oil into the muscles, first the lower leg and then the upper leg and thigh. He paid particular attention to the needs of the inside of the upper leg, but always ensuring that he never touched her most private area. Having massaged both legs in this way he could tell that the woman was highly aroused.

With a skilled and practised hand he soon removed her knickers. She offered no resistance to his manly dominance as he lifted her hips to assist in the removal. Having done so, he gently parted her legs before applying a little oil to their insides. He massaged this in with the gentle dexterity required of the moment, using just the index and middle fingers. Making small circular movements in this way he reached the very top of her legs and then proceeded to continue the massage over her private area.

She moaned softly as he touched her this way. As she moaned he pressed more firmly until he had located the precise spot that he wanted to touch. As he did so she gasped and then her body started to arch as she took her first pleasure of the night.

As her arching subsided Palmer undressed until he wore only his boxer shorts. Now he turned the woman over and kissed her passionately on her lips. Tongues entwined in the sweetness of the moment of passion. They stayed entwined as he explored her chest with a hand. He cupped his hand around the firmness of her breasts and gently rubbed the erect nipples until she started to moan again under his touch. He continued this way kissing and caressing her until she reached the second peak. As she did so he felt her writhing under his body, not for want of escape from the man, but from the pleasure that he was affording her.

Having peaked for the second time the woman decided it was her turn to give some attention. She reached out and touched the boxer shorts. She was evidently pleased with what she touched for she grabbed it firmly in her hand.

"Right darling, it's my turn. Turn over on your back." She whispered softly in his ear. Having satisfied her immediate cravings for release, she proceeded to repeat the treatment on him that she had just received.

She watched carefully as his excitement grew. She waited for the moment when he reached out and grabbed her and pulled her to him. She thrilled as he forced her onto her back. She felt his knees pushing her legs wide apart but by now she was lost in the pleasures of the night. She felt him pierce her, and she screamed out in pleasure, her nails digging into his back as she raked them over his flesh.

He thrust wildly into her with the energy of a teenager. Sweat broke out on both their bodies as they searched for the final release. Suddenly it was happening. Her body convulsed and her back arched at the same moment as he made his final thrust into her. She felt the result of his release deep in her own body and her pleasure passed slowly as they lay together still bonded but now relaxed.

After a minute Palmer kissed her tenderly on the lips. "Was that good for you, darling," he

157

whispered passionately, noting that her eyes were still closed.

"Hmm, the best."

Palmer gently withdrew from her body, still with the consideration and tenderness he felt for her. He lay there on his back beside her and reached out to hold her hand. Lying like this, the woman soon fell asleep. Palmer lay there, waiting, waiting for the moment that made him different to the other lovers she had known. He waited until he could hear the steady rhythmic breathing that told him she was deeply asleep.

Outside, the dark skies grew overcast and as the night drifted slowly by the rain began to fall, softly at first but as it grew harder Palmer stirred. She was breathing deeply now so he rolled over and touched her warm flesh. She in turn rolled into him and placed an arm over his shoulders. He in turn pulled her to him until he felt the warmth of her chest against his body. He reached an arm over her shoulder and began to gently stroke the nape of her neck. She stirred in her sleep, seemingly unwilling to awaken from slumber. Then he caressed her under the duvet. His free hand reached down to stroke between her legs. Stroking like this she was soon in the throes of awakening.

By now Palmer was significantly aroused himself. He was not perturbed when she rolled over and lay on her stomach. Instead he reached down and parted her legs before ministering his attentions to her for the second time that night. Still barely awake she moaned with pleasure as he continued to stir her into arousal. But for Palmer this would be very different to the earlier session. For now Palmer desired to satisfy her entirely. Sensing that she was aroused he lay on top of her, ensuring his manhood found the place that he had prepared. With force now he entered her, thrusting deeply into her semiconscious body. She offered no resistance to him as her own arousal grew.

Suddenly she felt his hands under her hips. In a moment he was forcing her to kneel as he knelt with her. Then he used the pressure on her hips to establish and maintain the steady rhythmic motion that he required. She melted under his dominance, allowing him to do whatever he wanted. This time though, with the earlier passions still affecting his body, Palmer took his time.

In so doing, he was able to give the woman the extended period of attention that he knew she really liked. He thrust forcefully into her for several minutes, always controlling the rhythm and depth of penetration through the hands that gripped her hips. By now she needed no assistance as she reached her own plateau of arousal.

He felt her tighten around him as she reached her peak, gasping loudly with each thrust that penetrated her body. He held her this way until she had peaked maybe five times. Palmer sensed that each peak happened slightly quicker than the previous one and he smiled to himself. He was completely in control and she knew it. It was, after all, what had made him so different to her other lovers.

As he continued to hold her this way, her mind drifted back to the first time they had euphemistically "slept together". She had had a string of lovers up until then, and each one had left

159

her feeling dissatisfied. Either they did not understand her needs or they simply didn't care, but it was always over in just a few minutes, the very point at which she was beginning to enjoy things. When she had gone to bed with Palmer that first time it had also taken him only a few minutes to satisfy himself and as he had rolled off her she had bitten her lip with the disappointment. However, after a brief rest he had turned to her and held her as he held her now. And she knew that he would carry on like this until she was satisfied. That was what had made him so different, and it had helped her to put up with some of his wiles and ways.

She felt him now as her muscles tightened in a spasm of pleasure. She felt the sure, controlled, rhythm that turned her wild. She felt him reach down and touch her just above the place where he had entered her. The point he touched was ultra-sensitive and as he stroked it gently she reached yet another peak. This was the end for her as her muscles went into what was seemingly a continuous spasm. She had reached the ultimate peak, the point from which it was impossible to go further, the highest of heights. And yet she knew he would keep her in this position for as long as he wanted.

And he wanted. He kept her there as she sobbed with joy, every muscle in her abdomen now caught up in the spasm of pleasure. He kept her there until she felt as if she had been run over by a steamroller. He kept her there for maybe ten minutes until he knew she could take no more of the pleasure. Then, and only then, did he release her from the position in which he held her. He pushed her legs even further apart and with just three deep thrusts he took his pleasure. After a few seconds he withdrew and let her fall back onto the sheets. Now totally relaxed she fell asleep without muttering a word. Covering her body with the duvet Palmer relaxed and slipped into the world of dreams.

***

Palmer made it back to his terraced house just before nine the next morning. The journey back from Karen's had been slow, the rush hour traffic being particularly heavy. As he entered the house he poked his head round the door to his office. He immediately noticed the rapidly flashing red light on the answering machine. Clearly somebody, or some bodies, wanted to speak with him. Palmer ignored the beckoning signal and made his way into the kitchen. He primed the precious coffee-making machine and then went upstairs. The sounds of music drifted down the stairs and into every corner of the house as he showered and then shaved. Finally, dressed casually for the day, he descended the stairs. He was in buoyant mood, as was often the case after an evening with one or other of his lady friends. He made his way back to the kitchen where the coffee was now waiting for him. Unhurriedly he made toast and poured the coffee into a large dark blue mug.

He took the toast and the mug into his office and pressed the play button. The answering machine announced,

"You have four new messages." There was a pause. The first piece of toast was maybe halfway between the plate and his mouth when the first message started.

"Damien, it's Eddie. Call me back when you have time. Bye." The machine sounded the electronic "beep" that separated messages.

"Mr. Palmer, this is Detective Inspector Kerrigan from Victoria police station. Please could you call me on the station number." The message continued with the number but Palmer ignored it as he watched the postman walk past the house. His attention was regained as the machine sounded another electronic "beep".

"Robert Mortimer here, could you ring me tomorrow morning as early as possible regarding some photographs? Thanks." Palmer stopped chewing at this message and made a note to ring his client.

"Hello, my name is Colin Haversham and I have been given your name and this number by a friend. I understand that you might be able to undertake a small assignment for me, with regard to having someone watched. If you could ring me back sometime I would be most grateful." Again the caller left his number and Palmer noted it down on the piece of paper on top of his desk.

It took Palmer a few minutes to finish the toast and drain the mug of coffee. When he had finished he picked up the phone and dialled Eddie Marston. He'd been first on the answering machine so he got Palmer's first attention. The phone rang, and rang, and rang. Finally a tired, groggy, voice answered it.

"Yeah."

"Eddie, it's me, Damien. How are you this morning?"

162

"Damien? Oh, Damien!" The voice registered the caller. "I'm not so good. Been up half the bleeding night. Thought you might have some work for me to do, that's all."

"I might have later on. How do you fancy a bit of surveillance?"

"Yeah, anything so long as it pays."

"Tell you what, give me half an hour and I'll call you back on it. Only I got a message from someone who wants something done, and it might be just up your street."

"Yeah, okay then, and thanks."

"You okay, Eddie?" Palmer's voice sounded concerned for his friend.

"Hmm, will be. Just a bit hung over. Had a bit of a night with some mates. Talk to you later."

"Yeah, I'll phone you back in about half an hour. Bye until then."

"Bye." The phone went dead as and Palmer looked at the notes he'd made from the other messages. He decided to ring the unknown Mr. Haversham. He dialled the number carefully and waited. A female voice answered.

"Hello."

"Oh good morning, could I speak to Mr. Haversham please."

"I'll just check if he's still in. Hang on."

Palmer heard the phone being placed down heavily on a hard surface. Then, in the distance, he heard the woman's voice.

"Are you still at home? There's someone on the phone for you?" There was a long pause before the phone was picked up once again.

"Hello, Colin Haversham speaking."

"Mr. Haversham, it's Damien Palmer. You called me last night."

"Oh yes. Thank you for getting back to me."

"Just before we go on, are you able to talk, or would you prefer to call me back some other time."

"Oh no, I can talk."

"Fine. Just thought with someone around you might not be able to. Carry on. How can I help you?"

"Well, I don't know really. Only, I think my wife is having an affair. She's started going out a lot, and coming back late at night. That sort of thing."

"And is that your wife who answered the phone?"

"Oh, good Lord no. That's the daily help. My wife left for work an hour ago."

"I see. Now, do you have any idea where she goes when she's out late at night?"

"None. But it's been going on for about three months now."

"And have you asked her what she's doing?"

"Of course I have, but she just makes up excuses. It's almost as if she wants me to try to find out."

"I see. Well, let's think. Probably best if we could meet up somewhere. Do you have a picture of her?"

"Yes."

"Good. Please bring it with you when we meet up. And also anything else you might think of as useful. For example, details of what kinds of clothes she wears. If she drives then I'll need details about the car, make, colour, registration number, that sort of thing."

"So you can help me?"

"Probably, but I'd like to talk to you about it face to face first. It's better than over the phone."

"Sure. When could we meet?"

"Depends. Whereabouts are you?"

"I live just off Wimbledon Common. Do you know it?"

"Certainly. What are you doing for lunch today?"

"Nothing planned."

"Excellent. Why don't we meet at the Dog and Fox in the village at say one thirty?"

"That's fine by me. Now, how will I recognise you?"

"I'll have a brown battered top-opening brief case. And how about yourself?"

"I'll be wearing a black puffer jacket and dark brown cords."

"Excellent. Well, Mr. Haversham, until one thirty then, and don't forget the picture and anything else you can think of."

"I won't and thank you. Goodbye now."

"Bye." The phone went dead. "Two down, two to go," thought Palmer as he weighed up which call to make next. He dialled the number and waited.

"Robert Mortimer please," he spoke when the receptionist answered the phone. Again the customary pause as he was patched through to his client's offices.

"Robert Mortimer, how can I help you?"

"Good morning Mr. Mortimer, it's Damien Palmer. You phoned me."

"I did. I was just wondering if I could have the photographs back. You asked me to give you forty eight hours, and well, that time is up, and I really do want to get this sorted out with my wife."

"I quite understand. Actually, I'm really hoping to have this all sorted out by tomorrow. Come to think of it, you having this out with your wife might just bring everything to a head. Can I drop them round later this morning?"

"That would be great. I'll see you sometime later on then."

"Assuredly. And thank you for being so patient."

"That's not a problem. Has it been of help to you?"

"Enormously, but I can't say much more just yet. I hope you understand."

"Naturally. Well, until later on then, and thank you."

"Until later on. Goodbye." For the third time the phone went dead. Palmer looked at the brief, terse, message he had noted down from D.I. Kerrigan. He wondered for a moment what service he might be to the Metropolitan Police, and was still trying to guess as he dialled the number.

"D.I. Kerrigan please," Palmer announced with a degree of authority when the female voice answered the call.

"One moment sir, I'll see if he is available. Who shall I say is calling?"

"Palmer. Damien Palmer. I'm returning his call, presumably from yesterday evening."

"Mr. Palmer, thank you, I won't keep you a moment. Please hold the line." The sound of the female voice was replaced with the awful strains of "canned" music so prevalent on telephone networks. After maybe a minute on hold Palmer was greeted once again by the female voice.

"Mr. Palmer, I'm sorry, but D.I. Kerrigan is in a meeting and can't be disturbed."

"Oh, well, in that case can you ask him to contact me, or should I ring back later?"

"I can leave him a message. Will you be on this number for the rest of the day?"

"No. Actually I'll be out and about quite a bit. Can I give you my mobile number?"

"That would be helpful." The distant female listened as Palmer read her out the number. When he had finished she repeated the number back for confirmation purposes.

"That's correct," Palmer commented after the number had been repeated. "And thank you."

"Good bye sir."

"Good bye." Palmer replaced the handset, none the wiser as to the purpose of the call. He paused for a minute looking at the additional notes he'd doodled while making the four calls. He formulated a plan in his mind and picked up the phone once again.

"Eddie?"

"Yeah. That wasn't half an hour."

"Yeah I know, but I have to go out. Can I pick you up about twelve thirty?"

"Why?"

"Got a client who wants some surveillance doing. Thought you might like to come to the meeting and pick up the details first hand."

"Oh, right. Well, yes." Marston sounded uneasy. Palmer decided it probably had more to do with a headache than any element of unease at the task ahead. After a pause Marston continued. "Twelve thirty then, I'll be ready. What's it about?"

"Not really sure yet, but it sounds like a case of the wife who plays away from home."

"One of them?"

"Yes. Could mean some sitting round not doing much, but then again it could be totally different. You interested?"

"Yeah. See you at twelve thirty."

"Okay then. Oh, and its casual. We're off to a pub in Wimbledon. Bye."

"Bye." Marston's farewell never reached Palmer's ear as he replaced the receiver before Marston had uttered the monosyllable.

Palmer wrote down a few rough notes on the piece of paper and checked his brief case. He looked quickly at his watch. It was just after ten o'clock, and it was time he paid the first of his calls that morning. Before leaving the house he double-checked the contents of the briefcase, ensuring that the plain manila envelope was intact. As he checked, he remembered with amusement the reaction of his client to the pictures that lay within the envelope. Palmer made the short walk to "Duggan and Mortimer Architects" in less than ten minutes. The same petite brunette was seated at the front desk though today, Palmer noticed, she was wearing blue/green nail varnish. He smiled and asked to see his client and in due course was ushered back into the same office he had been in a few days previously.

"Mr. Mortimer." The men shook hands as the brunette left them, closing the door firmly behind her.

"Mr. Palmer, thanks for coming. You have the envelope?"

"Of course, but just before I give it to you, you are sure this is what you want?"

"Positive. She's been using me for ages. This will just let me get back on even terms."

"So I take it your marriage is not on a firm footing at the present moment."

"You take it right, though I don't see what business that is of yours."

"None. None at all, just an observation, that's all."

"Oh, I see. The ever alert detective bit, is that it?" Mortimer smiled weakly.

"Something like that I suppose. It just seems a shame that's all."

"Shame?"

"Yes. Well, from what I've seen she's one in a million." Palmer reflected back to his visit to Sharon Mortimer's little beauty shop. He had to admit that she was attractive, and she had such wonderful hands. He remembered the facial she'd given him and the offer of a comprehensive list of services to her male clients. Palmer barely needed to guess what that might mean. It was actually true. She was one in a million. With what she was into she needed to be. He smiled slightly.

"Oh yes, she is. Not many women would help their husbands to virtually go bankrupt by selling off their secrets."

"Selling, you never said anything about selling?" Palmer sounded intrigued.

"Well, not directly. She'd just talk about them to her toy boy, but you can bet he sold them on to his brother. Like I said before, he needed the money."

"Before? I don't recall. Do enlighten me."

"Yeah, he needed the money. Derwent, that is the man you photographed, has a problem. John told me about it a couple of years ago. Apparently there had been this big bust up at John's offices one day. Simon, that's the guy in the pictures, had stormed into his brother's offices demanding money. There'd been this big scene about how the older brother had a duty to look after the younger one. Anyway it transpired Simon had a drink problem and had been heavily gambling, to the point where his creditors were about to turn nasty. According to John, his partner, Richard, had loaned Simon the money to pay off his gambling debts on the understanding that he sorted out the drinks problem and then repaid him the loan. Well, last I heard was that Simon still had a drinks problem but he'd started paying the money back, but I didn't know how at that point. Of course I do now – he's sold his brother the information he got from the two timing slut of a wife I got saddled with."

"And do you think he still needs money?"

"I don't know. Why?"

"Well, you might have an opportunity to get even with him."

"How do you mean."

"Well, let's see. Your wife sleeps with him and presumably she talks to him too, passing on information."

"Oh, she does more than that. She hands him bits of paper that he then photocopies, or just takes."

"Okay, so she gives him stuff too. Well, it shouldn't be too hard to sort out."

"I'm sorry, I'm not with you."

"Tell me, do you have any fairly big project on at the moment, something that might interest the likes of Derwent?"

"Yeah, there is one. Why?"

"Well, for Mr. Baker's sake, here is what you could do." With that Palmer set about explaining to his client what it was he could do. It took him nearly half an hour and at the end of it Mortimer sat back in his chair as if slightly stunned.

"Are you sure it would work?"

"I have absolutely no idea. But could you do your bit?" Palmer was mildly surprised at his own ingenuity. He genuinely had no idea if his plan would work, but it would certainly cause a stir.

"Yeah, from my point of view there isn't a problem. Just run a few simulations, it's all on computer. Change a few parameters and hey presto."

"Yeah, but it's got to look good."

"It will, don't worry. Now, those photographs?"

"Are you sure?"

"Positive. I want her to see them. I want her to run off to him, and I want her to give him what she can. Thank you Mr. Palmer, it's a brilliant idea. Now, if I am to succeed I must get on. There's a lot to do."

"Certainly. I must be on my way anyhow."

"I'll show you out." The two men stood and Mortimer courteously showed Palmer out of his office and through the front door. The two men shook hands before Mortimer let the door shut. He was smiling as he turned to the receptionist.

"Siobhan, please could you ensure that I am not disturbed for the rest of the day. I'll have something for you to do later on but I'll call you when I need you."

"Certainly Mr. Mortimer." She straightened up in her chair, looked straight at her employer and ensured that her body language conveyed her feelings for him. In return he smiled deprecatingly at her and walked back into his office. He closed and then locked the door before pulling down the blind. He was alone and secure in his office. He made one short phone call to his wife letting her know that he would be a little late home that evening but he hoped to have some good news for her. He did his best to make the conversation as relaxed as possible, though as he talked to her he scanned the pile of photographs he had received, photographs showing her in the most intimate of positions with another man. Finally Mortimer replaced the pictures in the envelope and went to work.

It took Palmer only a few minutes to walk back to his house. He had just entered the front door when the phone started ringing.

"Damien Palmer, how may I help you?"

"Mr. Palmer, glad I caught you in. It's John Nash. There's been a development. My colleague Mr. Goodland was found yesterday evening. A body was washed up at Hastings late yesterday. As he has no living relatives it fell to me to go and confirm his identity. According to the pathologist the body had been in the water for a couple of days. It was a mess, to say the least, and the police obviously think that it's foul play. There was nothing on the body to indicate what happened, no stab wounds, bullet holes or anything. The body was such though that anything else would have been impossible to determine."

"Oh God, that's awful. You say he had no relatives?"

"No, none, why?"

"I can't remember for the moment. Just something someone said to me a day or so ago. Can't remember it at the moment, and it's probably irrelevant anyway."

"One other thing Mr. Palmer, I told them about your mysterious phone call to Mr. Goodland, what was it, four days ago?"

"Yeah. What was their reaction?"

"Well, they want you to make a statement, of course, and as soon as possible."

"You mean I have to go down to Hastings?"

"No, no, we can make other arrangements for that."

"Thank God for that. I don't have time to go all that way, not right now. I think, very possibly, that it is time to speak to Miss Cavendish again."

"Again? But you only talked to her a few hours ago."

"I know, and in a few more hours I anticipate I will need to speak to her again. How about four o'clock this afternoon?"

"I'll see if she is available. And while you're here we could sort out your statement."

"Fine."

"In that case, I'll phone you back as soon as I have confirmed things with my client."

"Thanks. I'll be in for a while now."

"Right. Talk to you soon. Goodbye." The phone went dead. Palmer sat quietly for a few minutes chewing over the information he had just received. He had not the faintest idea why he wanted to talk to once again to Cavendish, it had all just come out on the spur of the moment. But there was no doubt in his own mind that something was worrying him about this case. Of course the mysterious death of his client's solicitor was bound to be purely coincidental. There was nothing, absolutely nothing that Palmer knew at this time to suggest otherwise. It had to be one of life's quirks of fate.

He sat at the desk looking at the blotter, his head propped up by the two linked index fingers that pushed up under his chin. Palmer was thinking, trying to see the wood for the trees. He still had an hour to go before he needed to pick up Marston. There was no preparation for that meeting needed. He'd done dozens, if not hundreds of the kinds of cases he was about to hear about. They were usually boring. He'd had the same thoughts about the Mortimer case when he Robert Mortimer had contacted him for the first time. That had been a few days before the visit from Cavendish. And now, just a few days later the two cases seemed inextricably linked, but there were still too many loose ends, and it was the loose ends that troubled Palmer for the better part of the next hour.

He thought about the link between Sharon Mortimer and the Derwent family and even Cavendish's own link to Richard Derwent. Then there was the business link between Cavendish and Sharon Mortimer. But that was purely business, and by Mortimer's own account Cavendish had little to do with the daily running of the business. Put it all together, Palmer thought with some amusement, and you ended up with business partners sleeping, or at least having slept with, brothers. Not really a case, and definitely not unique. But, Palmer thought, he was getting closer to providing Cavendish with the alibi she wanted. There had been some inconsistencies in the various accounts he'd heard of the events sixteen months earlier, differences that meant either someone was wrong, or someone was deliberately trying to mislead him.

He pondered the information he had to hand, his brain trying to untangle the mine of details. He began to formulate a few questions he would like to ask Cavendish when he met her later on that day. There'd been something about the meeting the previous afternoon, something about her demeanour that bothered him, and Palmer didn't like that particular feeling.

Finally he sat back in the swivel chair, closed his eyes and continued his deliberations. He knew from experience that he probably had all the information he needed to solve the case. Now all he needed to do was sort it all out and then he could set about the undoubtedly complex task of proving his theory.

Chapter 8

The telephone interrupted his concentration after nearly half an hour. Palmer heard it ringing and reacted slowly, so slowly that the answering machine intervened. He heard his by now familiar introduction and then the electronic beep indicating the caller could leave their message.

"This Is D.I. Kerrigan from Victoria ..."

The rest of the message went unheard as Palmer intervened by picking up the handset.

"Hello, Mr. Kerrigan, it's Damien Palmer. Sorry, but the machine beat me to it. How can I help you?"

"Mr Palmer, at last we meet, so to speak. I tried ringing the number you left the WPC but there was no response."

"Oh, sorry, the battery must have run out. I'll check it out, and thanks for pointing it out."

"That's okay. The reason for the call is that we are investigating a case of serious wounding, and during the investigations your phone number came up."

"Really?"

"Yes. Now of course we know who you are, and what you do, so do you mind if I am short and to the point?"

"No, fire away." Palmer sounded slightly more reticent and surprised that his fame had even reached the Met.

"Well, actually we got your number as being the last person to have called the victim of the wounding."

"I see, and who is that?"

"A Miss Jane Dervan," and as Palmer reacted in shock, the officer proceeded to mention the address, though Palmer was not listening. He recovered enough to hear the voice on the other end of the phone say, "Are you still there sir? Hello, are you there?"

"Yes I'm here. Sorry, after you mentioned her name I lost the rest. Is she all right."

"You do know the lady then sir?"

"Yes, I know her, we're actually good friends. Is she all right?"

"Why shouldn't she be sir?" The voice at the other end of the line was fishing.

"Only you mentioned a case of malicious wounding." Palmer reacted quite naturally, quite out of shock.

"Yes sir, I'm afraid she's been quite badly wounded."

"How badly? She will be all right won't she?"

"Too early to say sir."

"Where is she?"

"She's in the Westminster. But she is under guard and she is far too ill to see anyone yet. Do you know if she has any family who we can contact"

"Oh God, let me think. No, none that she's ever mentioned to me, and I've known her for about seven years now."

"I see sir, and when did you last see Miss Dervan?"

"Let's see now. Four nights ago, actually I stayed round at her flat. Left about eight the next morning."

"I see sir." The voice on the other end of the telephone line changed to a somewhat more sinister voice. "I think that in that case we'll need a statement from you. Would you mind coming over to the station today if possible."

"Today." Palmer was thinking hard. "It couldn't wait until tomorrow could it, only I have a meeting this afternoon?"

"We'd prefer to do it today."

"Okay then, but it will have to be later on, say about half past five."

"Very good sir, we are open all day and night too. If you'd be so good as to ask for me when you arrive at the station. Do you know where we are?"

"Oh yes. I'm actually quite well known to your Chief Superintendent. We, err, went to school together and stayed friends since."

"Right you are sir. Well, we'll expect you at five thirty, and thank you for your co-operation."

"Don't mention it Mr. Kerrigan. We are, after all, on the same side. Even if at times it doesn't seem like it." Palmer had noted that the D.I.'s voice had mellowed at the news that Palmer was acquainted with his boss.

"Until five thirty sir, goodbye."

Palmer replaced the phone on its cradle and digested the news. It took him a further five minutes to get ready for his next appointment and he was about to go out when the phone rang again.

"Mr. Palmer?" The voice was familiar to the sleuth.

"Mr. Nash, isn't it?"

"Yes. Bad news I'm afraid. I have been unable to contact Miss Cavendish. Of course she may have gone out shopping or something, but I thought you ought to know. I'll keep trying, but as time is marching on, you understand?"

"Yes, I understand. Well, how about first thing tomorrow. Say ten o'clock?"

"Should be okay, provided I can contact Miss Cavendish?"

"Does she not have an answering machine?"

"If she does have one it's switched off. As I said, I'll keep trying."

"Thanks. And if you do get any luck, can you ring this number and let my machine know. I'm off out now and I'll have to switch off the mobile phone for a bit."

"Oh right, let me just make a note of that." There was a pause as the solicitor made his note. "And we'll do your statement then as well."

"Yes, okay. Right, I must go. See you tomorrow at ten, unless I hear otherwise."

The phone went dead and Palmer made haste to exit the building before he could be interrupted again. He was now, almost predictably, running late for his appointment. He drove quickly to the home of Eddie Marston. It took nearly twenty minutes but at least, Palmer thought as he negotiated the traffic, he was heading in the right direction for the appointment. He also mused at how fate tended to have a hand in things. Having to move the Cavendish appointment to the next day gave him some time to think things through, and it also gave him time to go up to London, make his statement and then hopefully to go and see how Jane was.

Palmer's driving at the best of times was never sedentary, and this lunchtime it was less sedentary than usual. By the time he pulled up outside the grey building that housed eight converted flats he had almost made up the time he'd lost due to the phone call from Nash. He looked at the building with its grey walls with the dirty windows and felt a mixture of feelings. He felt sad that people had to live in such dreary buildings, packed in with barely enough room to call a home. But Palmer's sadness was mixed with a sense of admiration for his friend as he remembered the struggle, the almost titanic struggle that Marston had made to overcome illness. He remembered how Marston had come back from the very brink of death after he had been stabbed eight times. He remembered how any one of the stab wounds had only needed to be placed a few inches away from where it had landed and Marston would never have reached hospital alive. He remembered the weeks of touch and go hospitalisation, the care of the doctors and nurses and the gradual recovery. He remembered Marston's determination to get on with life, to pick up the pieces as best he could. And he remembered the day Marston had proudly showed him round his new flat. It was his, all bar the mortgage. He earned it, and he deserved it, and now whenever he could Palmer tried to help him by giving him the work that he loved and was so good at. As he remembered he pressed the car horn twice. In a moment Marston appeared in the doorway and with a grin sauntered over to the waiting car.

"Damien, how are you?" His greeting was uttered barely before the car door had opened.

"I'm okay. You remember Jane Dervan?"

"Course. Went and looked her flat over, what was it, three days ago." He stopped as he sensed the gravity of Palmer's voice.

"Well, she's been badly wounded. Had a call from the police just before I left. She's in the Westminster, can't be seen and apparently it's touch and go."

"She'll be all right Damien, she's tough. She'll be all right." There was genuine conviction in Marston's voice.

"Let's hope so Eddie. I have to go and talk to the police later on. Seems like I was the last to phone her. You sure she wasn't in when you called?"

"Yeah, yeah, I'm sure. I went and pressed the buzzer to her flat and got no response. Then I pressed another one next to hers and got this woman on the other end. Said I was her brother George. She said Jane had gone out in the morning and she'd not got back by that point."

"Yeah, I remember you telling me. Nothing else?" Palmer raised the question as he began to drive to the appointment."

"Nope. Just like I told you. Her flat was quiet and she didn't look like she was in. No lights on or anything."

"Hmm. Well, we'll see what I can find out later on."

With that the questioning was over and the two men chatted amiably as Palmer drove to Wimbledon Village. It was not a long drive and they arrived in the village at just after one fifteen. Palmer found a place to park alongside the common and stopped the car. The Common land that adjoins the Village is flat. There is a large, natural, and at times, almost empty pond that covers the central part of the flat land.

"Come on, it's nice out. We'll go and sit by the pond for ten minutes and I'll tell you what I know about the chap we're going to be meeting." Palmer picked up the brown brief case and having locked the car the two men walked briskly over to the bench that was situated some way back from the pond. The men looked out at the cold, grey, water. Tiny ripples on the surface of the water caused it to lap at the shore, the low water level indicating that the previous summer had been hot.

"Here, take this. It's my notes, such as they are." Palmer handed his friend a slim, clear, plastic, folder. It contained a single sheet of paper on which was scribbled a series of pieces of information.

Marston sat looking at the sheet for a couple of minutes, trying to unravel the sleuth's scribble.

"Seems straightforward enough," he said at last.

"Yeah. That's what we're here to find out. Let's hope so. Now, you let me do the introductions and start off the questioning. Then you join in when you want to."

"Fine by me."

Palmer and Marston walked the short distance through the village to the large pub on the corner by the stables. Palmer pushed open the door and strode purposefully to the bar. He ordered two pints of bitter and, once served, the two men went and sat at a table in the corner. Whilst Palmer had been ordering the alcohol Marston had taken a quick look round the pub and confirmed that their contact had not arrived. In fact it was a further five minutes before the door to the pub opened and a man wearing a black puffer jacket and dark brown cords entered. As he did so Palmer stood up and walked towards him.

"Colin Haversham?" Palmer completed his enquiry with a hand stretched out in greeting.

"Yes. Mr. Palmer I presume?"

"Indeed. Now, what will you drink? We have a table over there."

"We? I thought you would be alone."

"We can be if you prefer, but Eddie is an old friend and helps me out on these kinds of matters. So if you don't mind?"

"No, I don't mind at all. Mine's a pint of lager please."

"Won't be a minute." Palmer returned to the bar and ordered the lager. In a minute he was making the introductions at the table.

"Eddie Marston, meet Colin Haversham. Colin, just to let you know, Eddie is very good at surveillance, which is why I've brought him with me. Now, would you like to tell us what the problem is?"

And so Colin Haversham began to relate his fears. He told the detectives how his wife had started going out for the evening a couple of times a week about three months ago. He told them how she always dressed up and wore expensive perfume. He told them how he'd tried to follow her but how she had just disappeared. And finally he told them how when he had questioned her about it all she had been evasive and even told him some outright lies.

"And so, Mr. Palmer, it seems to me that she is having an affair. What I need is the evidence to prove it, and I understand you are one of the best at getting it."

"And how do you know that?"

"A friend told me, just a few days ago as it happens. I mean, of course he's known about my fears for a while now, but it was only a couple of days ago I started talking about getting a divorce. Anyway, he gave me your name and said you were good."

"And might I ask who the friend is?"

"Oh, Bob Mortimer. Apparently you did some work for him a while back, for which he is very grateful."

"Mortimer?" Palmer's tone of voice was deliberately enquiring and deliberately rhetorical. He was momentarily surprised by this revelation as well as intrigued. "Oh yes," he said after several seconds, "I remember now. Wasn't much of a thing from what I remember."

"Well it was to him."

"Glad to hear I have some uses. Anyway, to your own situation, and this is what I suggest. First off, I want you to leave your wife alone. On no account must you tell her about this meeting, nor must you show any further tendencies to question her about where she goes. Nor, and this is vital, must you attempt to follow her. She knows you, and your car, so you will just give the game away every time. What I suggest is you leave it to us, or more specifically to Eddie. He is a stranger to your wife and she definitely won't recognise his car. So leave the surveillance to Eddie. What I suggest is that next time you know she is out, you contact Eddie and he will follow her. We'll see where she goes and who knows we might get lucky."

"Sounds fair enough to me. But I don't want any harm to come to her, no dangerous stuff, you understand?"

"Perfectly. Eddie is not into dangerous stuff. Just a good old-fashioned bit of surveillance. She won't even know she's being watched, I promise."

"Okay." Haversham was sounding a bit more relaxed. "Now, how much will it all cost?"

"That's very difficult to say. For example, let's say that we follow her one evening and it takes say three hours to get everything sorted out. If we take that, plus expenses, pictures if appropriate and a summary report, I'd say you're looking at about two hundred quid. Of course, it might take a lot longer and, therefore, cost a lot more."

"Fine." Haversham was thinking as Palmer spoke. "There is one more thing. I know she is going out tonight at eight o'clock. Is there any chance you could follow her tonight?"

Palmer looked at Marston who nodded thoughtfully.

"Yeah," it was Marston who replied, "I can manage tonight. I'll need a picture, address, and her car registration to go on. That sort of thing."

Haversham turned to look at Marston. "I thought you would so I have it all here. Our address, her car make, model and registration. I have a picture of her here. It's about four months old and her hair is a bit shorter now. There's also my mobile number if you need to contact me for any reason. Anything I've forgotten?"

"One thing," Marston beat Palmer to the question, "do you have any idea where she goes or what she might be wearing?"

"Only that she heads off towards Sutton. I have to say that I've never followed her past the lights at South Wimbledon station. Done that three times now. As for what she wears. Well," and he thought hard for a moment. "She always wears knee length boots, dark brown. And she has this camel-coloured coat she takes with her. If it's cold she leaves wearing it, if not she just slings it in the car."

"Excellent."

"Do you want some kind of retainer for this?" Haversham looked at Palmer. As he did so he reached into his jacket pocket.

"No, not for now, if we get a result tonight we can probably sort it all out in the next day or so. If not, we'll see. After all, we know where you live." Palmer smiled warmly as Haversham withdrew his hand from the pocket inside his jacket.

"So, do you need anything else from me?"

"No, I don't think so. Another drink?" Palmer stood as if to return to the bar.

"No thanks, I must be getting back." Haversham stood also bade his farewells.

"Eddie, another pint?" Palmer turned to his friend once his client had left.

"Yeah, I'll get them."

"No need, it's on the company." In a couple of minutes Palmer returned with two more pints of bitter.

"Anyway," he said after taking the first sip from his new drink, "what did you make of our Mr. Haversham?"

"Not a lot really, though I can't say I blame his wife for going out. He comes across as a bit boring."

"That was exactly my feeling. Now tonight, are you sure about it?"

"Yeah. I'll get round there about seven thirty and hole up. If I take a recorder and a camera we should get this one sorted tonight. Who knows, she might just do evening classes."

"She might, but I doubt it. Anyway, cheers and good luck."

The two men sat and talked idly for several minutes as they drank the beer. Palmer had confidence in Marston and rightly so. Just as Palmer had truthfully told Haversham, Eddie Marston was extremely good at surveillance.

Their beer finished, Palmer drove Marston back to his drab, dreary, flat, before making his own way up to London and the equally dreary offices of the Metropolitan Police in Victoria.

***

It was much later, and the sun had long since departed below the horizon, when Eddie Marston left his flat and headed back toward the village of Wimbledon. His nondescript and slightly dented red Fiesta arrived at the common at just after seven in the evening. It was a cold evening though fine and Marston soon found the road he was looking for. Haversham's directions from the centre of the village had been good, and Marston soon found the address he was looking for. As he drove nonchalantly past the drive he noticed the gleaming white Peugeot hatchback in the drive. He smiled to himself and congratulated himself on firstly finding the address and also being in time. He parked his own car about fifty metres down the road. His parking looked casual but it was anything other than that. He'd turned the car round so that he was now looking directly up the road towards the driveway he'd passed. From the details Haversham had given him it seemed likely that the woman would pull out of the drive and head back towards the village, away from him. If she did as was expected, then he would have no trouble in following her. The greatest risk of losing her would, Marston reckoned, be at the main junction into the village. It was a risk, and one he could not avoid. If, however, she turned out of the drive and passed his own car, Marston had calculated that he could turn the car round in a matter of seconds. His calculation was based on the fact that he had parked directly opposite a wide driveway, one that he could use to turn the car round in a single, tight, circle.

Marston reached forward to the glove compartment and pulled out a map of the area. He studied it for the third time since the meeting with Haversham. Many of the major roads were now familiar names to him. His almost photographic memory had long since recorded the essential details of the layout of the various junctions. He studied the map, keeping one eye on the road ahead of him, just in case. It was just after seven fifteen.

***

The day had passed swiftly for Robert Mortimer. He had had much work to do, and it had all gone smoothly. In fact, it had gone so smoothly that he had deliberately sat in the office for some time after he could have gone home. He did so because he'd earlier phoned his wife to say that he would be a bit late. And so he had sat around. Long after his secretary had knocked on the door to say she was leaving for the day, Mortimer sat at his desk. In front of him was the manila envelope, and on top of the envelope lay the dozen pictures of his naked wife cavorting in an open sexual act with another man. The anger had passed and Mortimer had complied with Palmer's suggestions. Now the pictures lay on the desk as Mortimer rehearsed in his mind the events that would take place that evening.

His earlier telephone call had assured him that his wife would be at home. In all probability she would be wearing something alluring as she always did when he suggested there might be good news. That meant she'd help him relax, as only a wife should do. Once relaxed she'd gently get him to start talking, and then, when she'd got out of him what she wanted, like as not she'd decide to go out. Only now, in the midst of the current events, did Mortimer recall how many times it had been like this. Only now did he understand the reasons. Only now, as he looked at the pathetic pictures in front of him, did he fully understand what her motives were.

Beside the pictures lay a sheet of paper. On it were written a string of numbers, digits that when combined together made up a telephone number. It was a number that Palmer had left him that morning. It was part of the plan.

Mortimer scanned the pictures again. The man was not particularly well endowed and it intrigued Mortimer that his wife should find the man attractive. But then again, he reasoned, if Palmer was right, attraction was not the motivation in this instance. If Palmer was right, and it seemed a pretty big "if", then the motivation was more to do with money, and if that were the case, it could be argued that Palmer might have saved Mortimer's life. There was only one catch – Mortimer still had to face the evening, and if Palmer were right, he would have to do so with infinite caution.

At a little after six in the evening he replaced the pictures in the envelope and added a single sheet of paper on which he had added a hand-written message. He sealed the envelope and picked up the report that he had been working on ostensibly all day. He turned out the light and closed up the office for the day. As he locked the door and walked down the street he looked back with the kind of look that indicated this could be his last day at the office.

He drove home to Sutton, arriving shortly after six thirty. The hall light was on as he turned the key in the latch. Stifling the immediate thoughts of hate that flooded his mind he turned the key. As he did so the woman who was his wife appeared at the kitchen door.

"Hi, darling," she called out before he'd had a chance to enter the house. "Busy day?"

"Yes. Had to finish off the prep work for a big contract we've picked up. I've brought it home to have a look at in the morning before I go in. I'm too tired to do it tonight."

The woman was indeed dressed alluringly. Even as Mortimer saw her for the first time that evening he had to bite his lip when he thought her dress was meant for someone other than himself.

"You look nice," was about the best he could muster.

"Thanks. Why don't you go and have a shower? Dinner will be about twenty minutes. She turned to go back into the kitchen and Mortimer caught a glimpse of her breasts silhouetted under the fine black silk dress she was wearing. She was clearly wearing no underclothes. Again he had to hold back from expressing his feelings. He left the report and the envelope on the newel post and went upstairs. The shower was hot and the powerful spray of water on the back of his neck soon started to relax him. On a normal evening this would have been sufficient to help him unwind but tonight, with Palmer's warning fresh in his mind, he failed to reach the point of relaxation.

A few minutes after climbing the stairs he descended them, dressed casually for the evening. The piece of paper that contained the all-important telephone number was safely hidden in a place where Mortimer was reasonably sure his wife would not look.

"Dinner is on the table," Sharon Mortimer called from the kitchen. "Your favourite – steak."

"Thanks darling." Mortimer had practised this next step carefully. He entered the kitchen and in his usual way went up to his wife and put his arms round her. She turned, still held by him, and their

191

lips met. Such was his apparent passion that she failed to notice his deception.

"Hey, big boy, you're keen. Let's eat first, I'm starving."

"If you say so, say, this looks good." Mortimer sat at the table and began to eat his meal. He had little appetite, and what appetite he did have was a result of Palmer telling him to skip lunch. Mortimer ate, slowly and carefully. His wife ate too and their conversation, as usual, was kept to a minimum.

"So, what's this good news then?" She asked him when the first course was nearly eaten.

"Oh, we've just secured a provisional contract for a bridge design. Worth a lot of money –so should be a good end to the year."

"So why is a provisional bridge design worth so much, darling?" Mortimer thought her interest was just a little too intense.

"Well, it's a pretty radical design. Could save loads on the construction costs and if we get it patented then we'd stand to make a fortune in the future. Thing is, I've got to get a copy of the report and the calculations to the client in the morning. So, just to ensure they go ahead with it we drew up some models on the computer. That's what's in the envelope. Those models won't half turn some heads when the client gets to see them I can tell you." Mortimer was almost sounding jovial.

"Dessert?" His wife smiled falsely across the table.

"Not for me, thanks, that was a real plateful. Don't think I could eat another mouthful."

"Okay. I'm pretty full too. Why don't you go and put the telly on and relax with a brandy or something. I'll bring some coffee in. Looks like you could do with a massage."

"Well," said Mortimer, now on his guard against her schemes, "I certainly wouldn't say no to any of that."

"Okay, I'll just clear these things away while the percolator's working. Be about five minutes." Sharon Mortimer busied herself round the kitchen as her husband retired to the lounge and the television.

From the comfort of his armchair in the lounge Mortimer could hear the gentle plop-plopping sound of the percolator as the coffee was brewed. He could also hear other sounds, sounds of his wife tidying up in the kitchen. After a couple of minutes she entered the lounge carrying two cups of the coffee. She placed them on the coasters that lay on the coffee table.

"Do you want a brandy?" she asked, sweetly.

"Yeah, all right, just a small one, and thanks." Mortimer looked up from the chair to his wife as she went over to the cocktail cabinet. She poured two brandies that were anything other than small. Mortimer was still watching her as she walked back and handed him a glass.

"You really do look quite wonderful tonight," he said, almost with affection.

"Eric Clapton eat your heart out." She laughed.

"Sorry?" Mortimer sounded confused.

"It's just the title of one of his songs. You almost got it right," she responded.

"Oh. Didn't mean to." Mortimer feigned defeat. He sipped the brandy and then looked at it appreciatively. He sat there with the glass obscuring his view of the television for several seconds. "A really nice one, that," he finally said as he turned to look at his wife. With a degree of surprise he noticed her glass was almost empty. She was not usually such a quick drinker of spirits yet he recalled almost instantly she did have a habit for such actions just before she would go out on some pretext or other.

"And is your coffee to your liking too?" she almost whispered, almost seductively.

By way of response, and without any thought Mortimer placed the brandy glass on the low table and picked up the cup of coffee. He took a sip. It was not particularly hot, so he took a larger mouthful.

"Yes, it's fine," he said as soon as he'd swallowed the mouthful. "Why?"

"Oh, they're just a different selection of beans to what we usually have," she replied. Mortimer was aware that she seemed to be watching him intently. He realised why too late. He began to speak.

"Well, now that you come to mention it, they do taste a bit bitter," he started. The sentence went unfinished, for the whole world began to spin. In his rapidly fading field of vision the room began to rotate. Suddenly there wasn't just one room, but two, and then three. The room was spinning, spinning, spinning, until Mortimer could take no more of it. Even as he reacted, he dropped the cup and the remainder of the contents fell to the floor. He closed his eyes as sweat began to break out on his forehead. "Poison," he gasped.

"Not quite, a hypnotic actually," she responded as he slumped back in the chair. "Now, you will do exactly what I tell you to do." She spoke quite authoritatively as she came and stood in front of him. She reached out and took his hands in hers. "Don't open your eyes it will make you feel sick. Just take my hands and we'll go up to bed. That way you can sleep it off."

Mortimer, sure that he was dead, yet somehow still able to move, took hold of the hands that he could not see. Gradually he managed to stand up. With his eyes shut the room seemed quite still. The hands led him out of the lounge and up the stairs into his bedroom. He lay on the bed feeling helpless. He was aware that one by one he was being divested of his clothes but he was powerless to resist. He was also powerless to resist his wife's attentions. His mind was now so confused that he could not be sure if this was genuine affection being shown him, or some wicked game in which he was the victim. He lay there as she caressed him. He felt her hands all over his body, teasing him, stroking him. Even in his semiconscious state he could not help but rise to the occasion. She continued for some time. When she had finished she stood back to admire her handiwork.

"And now I have a little surprise for you," she said as she straddled his stomach.

He could feel her on top of him but he could not summon up the energy to resist her. He felt his hands being raised above his head, and he felt her tying them to some part of the headboard. Then he felt her climb off him, only to return a moment later.

195

"Now, when I go out, it's my business. What I do is nothing to do with you," she started. As she did so, she started to caress him again. In his aroused, though semiconscious, state Mortimer began to moan. It was a moan that was partly due to his arousal and partly due to the fact that as the effect of whatever drug he had taken was beginning to wear off, his mind was beginning to think. And as he thought, he realised how easily he had been duped.

"And so, my dear husband," she was obviously agitated, "I am afraid that I have to do something to get my own back." Her voice was almost playing with him, almost mischievously. "I don't like nasty snooping people watching my every move. Nor do I like it when you use my friends. So now, you will have to pay the price." She walked away from him then and returned to blindfold him, though Mortimer had not yet dared to open his eyes.

Then Mortimer heard a sound, a sort of whirring sound. At first it worried him, but it was quiet and some distance away from the bed. He felt more reassured when his wife came and sat back on the bed beside him. He felt her hand continue what it was doing and in a few seconds his concern had given way to greater arousal. It was true that she was very good at massage, and it was evidently having the desired effect on the man. So much so, that her ministrations were over in less than two minutes. Even as Mortimer reached the peak of his arousal and the result of his excitement splashed onto his stomach, his wife stood up and a moment later the whirring sound stopped.

"Now", she started, "I've only just begun my little game. I'm off out for a bit now, but I'll be back in about two hours. You can stay right here where you are, and when I come back we'll talk some more."

"What snooping people?" His attempt was almost pathetic. He realised she'd known about it all the time, but he didn't know how.

"That fucking dickhead you've had follow me, that's who!"

"I don't know what you're talking about?"

"No?" she sneered at him. "Well I hope he gave you some good information, because it was the last you're going to get. Now I'm late, so it'll have to wait for when I come back later and get my things."

"Get your things?"

"You can hardly expect me to fucking stay here when all you do is spy on me." As she spoke her voice rose to a crescendo. As she finished she turned on her heels and stormed out of the bedroom and slammed the door. The window of the bedroom was open, and in the silence that followed her leaving the house, and in the darkness caused by the blindfold, Mortimer began to feel the chill night air on his naked body. He struggled with the cuffs around his wrists but to no avail.

It took him several minutes of writhing on the bed to loosen the blindfold. Finally, he succeeded in removing the cover from one eye. Now he looked around the room as if trying to locate the source of the whirring sound. It took only a few seconds. The video camera was sat on its tripod in the corner of the room. With dismay Mortimer noticed that the cassette housing was open and empty. The bitch, he

197

reasoned, had filmed him and taken the production with her. Mortimer laid back, his mind overwhelmed with what had happened. Again he struggled with his bonds and managed to turn over to at least see how he had been tied to the bed. He looked at the knots in the silk scarf and began to tug at one of the knots. Slowly, very slowly he began to work it loose. It was tiring for him and in the position he had to adopt his neck was extremely uncomfortable.

Several minutes later, and with his neck complaining about the pain, he managed to release a hand. From then it took only a few seconds to complete his release. Quickly he ran across the landing. He looked down the stairs and noticed the file and envelope had disappeared from the newel post. He smiled to himself. It wasn't exactly a smile of contentment for somewhere along the way he had seriously underestimated his wife's hatred of him, but at least she had taken the bait with her, so it was fair to assume she was at least partly following Palmer's plan. It was just a shame that she had taken the videocassette too. That changed things. It changed things quite significantly. He looked anxiously at his watch. It was nearly nine o'clock.

***

By seven fifteen that evening Marston was watching and waiting. He didn't have to wait for long. As the clock in the car moved to show the half-hour, ahead of him the white Peugeot pulled out of the drive and, as he had hoped, drove away from him. In a moment Marston was in pursuit. As the car had pulled out of the drive he'd caught a glimpse of the driver in the streetlight. It was enough to convince him that she was the same person that was in the picture that reposed on the passenger seat.

Marston followed her carefully. He judged that she was not in a hurry, her driving was steady and she showed no indication that she suspected she was being followed. From the house near Wimbledon Village, the woman journeyed down through Wimbledon itself and on towards Morden and Sutton. Marston kept a reasonable distance behind her. He knew the first part of her expected journey and he relaxed a little as he concentrated on the evening traffic.

She drove on, and judging by her head movements she was singing along either to a tape or the radio. It suited Marston that she was preoccupied. It probably meant she wasn't paying too much attention to the traffic in her rear view mirror. Marston followed her through the outskirts of Morden, and onwards to Sutton. He'd listened to Palmer earlier. At the very start of Sutton there is a large roundabout. Under the control of various sets of traffic lights it links no less than five major routes. Accordingly, as they headed for this roundabout Marston drove closer to his target.

It should have been of no surprise to Marston, but it almost caught him unaware, when she continued on the roundabout past the Sutton exit, and instead turned onto the road that Marston knew as the Sutton by-pass. Once past the junction the woman reached over to the passenger seat and picked up something. In the light of a street lamp

199

Marston observed that she was now talking on a mobile phone. The conversation was short, less than a minute, before the phone was once again on the passenger seat.

By this time the cars were nearing the village of Cheam and Marston was being very careful. He had, after all, followed her for several miles, and it would take only a moment of recognition for his cover to be blown. At the same time, he was now in unfamiliar territory and there was no indication from the client as to which way the person driving the car in front of him might go. So Marston made a decision. In between the junctions, the sets of traffic lights, and the various slip roads, he pulled back a reasonable distance. When a major junction was imminent he gently eased his own car several metres closer to the target vehicle.

Without warning the woman pulled into the right filter lane that directed traffic towards the village of Cheam. Marston was ready and followed her with a good deal more safety in mind than had been shown by the woman. The filter light was at red and Marston had no choice other than to pull up directly behind the woman. As she waited at the lights she appeared to be applying some kind of make-up. Still waiting for the lights to change to green, she combed her short, dark, hair. Then, just as quickly as she had pulled into the filter lane, she was on the move again.

To Marston it seemed that suddenly she had decided to take evasive action. Her speed through Cheam village was unnecessarily fast, and Marston decided it unwise to pursue her too closely. At the next lights she was turning right even as Marston came round the corner. The traffic lights were turning from green to amber. Normally Marston would have slowed to a halt, but his target was already halfway across the junction. Instead he accelerated to beat the lights. The amber was turning red even as Marston crossed his own line. Slamming down the brake pedal he just made the corner, but not before a car waiting to his left had sounded its horn in disgust at his actions. Guilt was something Marston didn't like the feel of, but his mind was now too focused on the car in front for the pain of the guilt to last for long. Sweat broke out on his forehead. He sighed, a big, relieved sigh.

"Getting too old for this fucking life," he muttered to himself. "That was too bloody close for comfort."

He continued to pursue the vehicle ahead of him, glad that the speed of the pursuit had been restricted by other traffic. The woman in the driver's seat ahead of him seemed agitated as she approached the vehicles ahead of her. It was just as if she were impatient at not being able to get to her destination quickly enough, which was probably the case.

Finally, after a few more junctions, she pulled into the kerb. She didn't indicate, she just stopped the car. Marston, suddenly far too close to her, had no choice but to continue his journey. To his right was a sort of park that looked like it contained a children's play area. Some way down the road was a turning that doubled back on the narrow piece of open space. Marston turned the corner and crawled his way back up the road. The white Peugeot was easy to spot, parked as it was on the opposite road.

Marston pulled up at a point where he had a good view of the car. The driver of the white Peugeot was locking the car, and Marston watched her walk to the front door of the house outside which she had parked. After a few moments the hall light in the house was turned on. A few moments later and the door opened. Marston was ready with his camera, but there was nothing worth photographing. The light was poor, and through the viewfinder Marston did not even catch a glimpse of whoever was inside the house.

He waited until the front door was shut before exiting his own vehicle. Nonchalantly he ambled back up the road he had just driven down, and then turned back onto the main road. He walked casually down the road, slowing slightly as he approached the Peugeot parked on the other side of the road.

There was other activity in the road that night. It was now nearly eight thirty and just as Marston was walking down the road a light coloured car roared up the road and pulled up in the road a few doors up from Marston's own target. The driver opened the door and swung herself out onto the pavement. She was not particularly tall, and had short hair. She was obviously in a hurry and wasted no time in half-running to the door of the house. Marston made a note of the incident, just as Palmer had taught him to do. After all, he had been told, you never know when a detail might be important, even if it seems totally irrelevant at the time.

Marston turned his attention back to his own mission. The front door was clearly shut and the hall light had been extinguished. Behind the gate was a plaque. Marston crossed the road to take a look at the inscription. For some reason it did not surprise him to note the owner of the property was a practitioner in alternative medicine. The list of therapies offered included the usual homeopathy as well as various others that Marston did not recognise. One thing was certain though, whatever therapy had brought Jane Haversham to this house on this particular evening it almost certainly was alternative, at least to her husband.

Marston crossed back over the road and leaned against the railings that protected the children's play area. He lit a cigarette and puffed gently.

"And what if she comes out in a hurry?" The voice behind him made him jump. In fact it made him choke on the smoke he had inhaled. When he had finished coughing he turned round.

"Damien, you bugger. You scared me half to death. What are you doing here?"

"Not the same as you, that's for sure. Why are you here?"

"Jane Haversham, I followed her here. Got here about fifteen minutes ago. You see that place over there with the board outside it. She went in there. Some alternative therapy centre apparently. Didn't actually see him, but the board tells you what he's into."

"Quite. And you know for sure it's a male, do you?"

"Well, no."

"Exactly. It could be a woman. Anyway, that was a pretty good bit of surveillance to follow her this far."

"So what are you doing here, and how did you get on with your Jane?"

"Got up there and made a statement. Waste of time really. She came round this afternoon and told them all about it. Gave them a description as well. They gave me a copy of the photo-fits. Here."

Palmer fished into his jacket pocket and pulled out two photo-fit pictures.

"I said I'd keep my eyes open. You don't recognise them do you?"

"No. But they're an ugly couple aren't they. So why are you here?"

"Just a hunch." Palmer stopped for a moment as if deciding just what to divulge. "Just up the road, let's see, one, two, three, four doors, lives a certain gentleman I'm interested in, and if I'm right he's going to be getting a certain lady visitor pretty soon."

"You're too late Damien. She arrived about ten minutes ago. I was walking down the road when that light coloured car over there pulled up. She dashed out of it and shot into the house. Didn't really pay too much attention to it. Some tall, thin guy opened the door."

"That car, you say. But that's not hers, unless she's got two cars. Wait here."

Palmer quickly crossed the road and ran the four houses up the road to the light coloured car. He peered in through the window briefly before running back to where Marston continued to lean against the railings, a fresh cigarette glowing between his lips.

"Not my target's, but it does look familiar somehow. So how's it going?"

At that point Marston straightened slightly. His casual glances across the road would have given the most perceptive of observers that he was in fact closely watching the house into which Jane Haversham had entered. Now, his casual glances became more focused. The hall light was turned on briefly, followed by the upstairs landing light.

"Looks like it's action time. Shame I can't get a view in the window." Marston was looking round him.

"There's a slide in the kiddies area if that's any use," said Palmer, recalling his photographic session from the same slide a few days earlier.

"Cheers mate, how do you know that?"

"Just good observation, and years of experience." Palmer lied, but as he did so he laughed quietly to himself. "And it's just typical that we both end up in the same street watching two women doing this stuff. Okay, you need the pictures this time, so make the most of it."

"Cheers, see you later."

"Go on, get on with it."

Marston left Palmer and in a moment was scaling the slide. The house attracting Marston's interest was not so directly opposite the slide as the house Palmer had been observing a few nights previously, but the view through the viewfinder of his camera was adequate. The curtains in what appeared to be the master bedroom were not closed and the wall was covered in mirrors. The woman was on the bed, still partly clothed. Marston could clearly see that she was posing. The other person in the room was fully clothed. The person had short dark hair and was evidently also female. Apart from the bed and the usual furniture one would expect to find in such a room, there was also a tripod on which rested what looked to be a professional piece of photographic equipment. The woman was standing behind the camera taking pictures. Marston recognised her as his target for the evening. Slowly the woman on the bed, who Marston did not recognise, began to undress. She unbuttoned her blouse and exposed her breasts. A few minutes later her short skirt had also been discarded. A few minutes later she was totally naked. All the time, the woman behind the camera continued to take pictures.

This was an unexpected turn of events for Marston. He hadn't seen Jane Haversham enter the building carrying anything remotely big enough to be that camera. Then, after a few more minutes of the nude on the bed posing, and a few more pictures having been taken, the two women changed positions.

The woman behind the camera remained totally naked. She was, thought Marston, quite pretty. Now the woman on the bed began to undress. As she did so, Marston continued to take his own photographs. It took several minutes for Jane Haversham to completely undress. Her movements were somewhat more clumsy than her partner's had been, but her body was, if anything, the more attractive. Finally the two women were entirely disrobed. The woman behind the camera now joined Haversham on the bed. They looked as though they were laughing at some joke or other. After a while they began to caress each other. Marston was unaware of the black VW golf that had parked in the road just opposite him. He remained unaware for some minutes as he watched the women caressing each other.

"Eddie, I need you down here. Have you got enough yet?" Palmer's voice filtered up to Marston.

"Yeah, what's up?" It took him a few moments to respond and he reluctantly averted his gaze to Palmer.

"My case has turned up. That's her Golf down there. Can you see anything going on, only the light's on upstairs."

Marston turned his attention to the house opposite and looked through the viewfinder.

"Not a thing, there's no one up there as far as I can see. Why?"

"Well, there's something not right. I figured the Golf would turn up, but you say that a woman's already gone in there. What did she look like?" Palmer was now standing directly beneath the slide and his voice was a loud whisper.

"Can't say for sure. Not particularly tall. Short hair, I'd say. And she was in a hurry."

"Right, we need to abandon your case for tonight, this is more important. Come down, I need some help." Marston took less than ten seconds to climb down the slide.

"Right," continued Palmer when Marston had reached ground level. "Did you get some evidence?"

"Yeah, but it's not what you think."

"That doesn't matter. I'll take the camera and develop the film. You can give me an E-Mail report tomorrow. For now though I need an extra set of wheels. There are three people in that house now. At some point at least two of them will be leaving, I

207

think. There's the driver of the Golf, the driver of the Fiesta, and there's the bloke in the house. Now, something you need to know. The bloke and the driver of the Golf are having an affair. I have no idea why the Fiesta driver is here, or who she is. Not from your description. I have one idea, but it's pretty absurd. When the Golf driver comes out I want you to follow her. She doesn't know you, but she does know me. I'll take whoever else comes out. Now where are you parked?"

"Just over there." Marston pointed to his car the other side of the play area.

"Excellent. You'd better get back there and be ready. She drives like a bat out of hell."

"Cheers, that's just what I need, another mad dash. Haversham's pretty fast too when she wants to be."

"Yeah, it's in their genes I think. Anyway, we'd best get ready. If I'm right, there'll be some action here pretty soon.

Marston and Palmer returned to their cars and waited. The minutes ticked by, and turned into an hour. An hour became an hour and a half. As it did so, Marston observed Jane Haversham come out of the house she had visited and return to her own vehicle. She drove off after a moment and silence returned to the street. It was now nearly ten thirty. For a while it seemed to Palmer that his hunch had only been partly right. What if Mortimer had decided to spend the entire night at this house? It could be a long wait. Then again, he asked himself in the quietness of his own car, who the other woman might be. The car looked familiar to him.

Then, just as the door to the house opened the penny dropped.

It dropped so loudly, to Palmer, that it was more like a resounding bell. Cavendish!

As the woman came out of the house it was immediately obvious that Palmer was right. Cavendish! But what was she doing there? Unless she'd come round to the house to sort something out. Perhaps it had something to do with her row the previous evening with the other Derwent brother. Palmer watched as Cavendish reached up to kiss Simon Derwent good-bye. He could not see anyone else at the doorway. Presumably Mortimer was still sitting in the living room, waiting for Derwent to turn his attentions to her. As Cavendish lingered a moment on the doorstep, Palmer picked up his mobile and dialled a number.

"Eddie, it's Damien. Looks like I'm on the move. You wait for the Golf. If the light goes on upstairs ignore it. I just want that Golf followed, got it?"

"Yeah."

"And if the chap comes out, name's Simon Derwent, instead, then follow him. I have no idea what he drives."

"Sure thing."

"Cheers then, and good luck." Palmer turned off the mobile and started his car. Cavendish was now getting into the light coloured Fiesta. Palmer noted that she fumbled with the car key when unlocking they door. She looked somewhat agitated. Her lack of composure intrigued the detective.

She drove off and Palmer followed her as she headed in the general direction of Wimbledon. The journey took about thirty minutes and they finally arrived outside the block of flats where she lived. As she alighted from the car she turned to look up the road where Palmer had stopped. As she did so, Palmer caught sight of her face in the streetlight. She looked old, as if she had received a terrible shock. Her forehead was furrowed with lines of anxiety. She wasted no time in looking. In a moment she had turned back and as she did so her coat opened up so that Palmer could see the fawn cardigan underneath. In that precious moment he saw something else, something that attracted his fullest attention – blood. At least that was what it looked like. A large patch of something covered the front of her cardigan, its dark sanguine colour clearly visible against the much paler background. It was a fleeting glimpse but it did not go unnoticed.

As she went indoors Palmer reached out and retrieved his mobile phone from the passenger seat. He pressed a couple of buttons.

"Eddie?"

"Yeah," came the equally terse reply.

"Where are you?"

"I'm still outside the house. There's been no movement. No lights have gone on upstairs either. Nothing."

"Right. Well, I'm back outside Cavendish's house."

"What the hell are you doing there?"

"She was the driver of the Fiesta. Recognised her as soon as she came out. Look, I think she had something down the front of her. It was dark, like blood."

"I didn't see it when she came out," Marston protested.

"Yeah, it was under her coat, on her cardigan or something. Look it might have been something else, but it just looked like blood. Are you sure there's nothing going on there."

"Nope, nothing."

"Right, well I have another call to make. I'll ring you back in about five minutes."

"Okay." Palmer broke the connection and dialled another number.

"Mr. Mortimer, it's Palmer, Damien Palmer. Sorry to trouble you so late at night. Can we speak?"

"Sure Palmer, she's still out. Don't know where she is do you?" Mortimer sounded tired and angry.

"Did everything go according to plan at your end?"

"If you mean, did she take the report and the pictures then yes. If you mean is that all she took, then no. She's got a videocassette on her that contains some very embarrassing footage. She basically drugged me and then took advantage. Doubtless lover boy will use it as blackmail."

"Not if you have done everything I've asked you to. Anyway I expect we'll be able to recover the cassette for you. Now, have you heard from your wife since she went out."

"No, and by now I should think she'll be staying out for the night."

"Possibly. If she calls you, will you let me know? It could be useful."

"Oh, and where are you?"

"I'm at Wimbledon. I got called to another urgent matter, but I have a colleague watching your wife and he will contact me if he needs help."

"Oh. So where is he?"

"I don't know for sure actually. Last I heard was when he was following your wife away from your home. Should hear from him shortly. I'll let you know if I hear anything. Must dash."

"Oh, okay then, and thanks for the call."

"And don't worry Mr. Mortimer." Palmer continued, lying, something that he was becoming good at. He might not have wanted Mortimer to worry, but that was exactly what he was doing at that precise moment.

The mobile phone rang.

"Damien, it's Eddie.

"Eddie, what's up?"

"Something, and maybe nothing, but I've been trying to get you for a couple of minutes. Soon as you put the phone down this small, dark coloured car turned up. Can't tell the make. Anyway two blokes got out and went up to the house we're interested in. They're in there now."

Back in his own car Palmer was listening intently to his colleague. The description of the car and the two occupants sent alarm bells ringing.

"Eddie, this is important. Forget what I said about following the VW. Whoever comes out of there first, follow them."

"Right, I'm on my way. The two blokes have just come out. Better go. I'll call you later."

The line went dead as Palmer sat back in his own car. Up in the flats the lights of number seven were still burning. It was now fast approaching midnight and Palmer wondered when the woman would go to bed. Not much later, he hoped, for she had an appointment with her solicitor the next morning, or at least he hoped she had.

As if in answer to his hopes the lights were extinguished one by one until only the bedroom light was left burning. Then, after a minute, it too was turned off and Cavendish's flat was bathed in darkness. Palmer waited. He waited ten minutes to be sure that Cavendish was not about to leave the flat again. Ten minutes later his own fatigue and the logic of the situation finally convinced him that Cavendish was home for the night. He yielded to both the powerful forces that were working against his desire to continue surveillance and began the journey to his own home.

Midnight passed and eventually Palmer arrived at his own doorstep. He let himself into the house and noticed that the light on his answer-phone was flashing a steady, rhythmical, beat. He pressed the button and listened to the short message from John Nash telling him that the appointment with Cavendish was arranged for ten thirty in the morning. He took the mobile phone and went upstairs. Tomorrow, he guessed, was going to be a long day.

Just before retiring he phoned the hospital in London where Jane Dervan lay recovering from her injuries. The news was good. It needed to be. Somewhere in this miserable business Palmer needed some good news. The fact that she was conscious and able to talk was good news. He promised himself that the next day he would visit her, once this case had been resolved.

Chapter 9

Palmer did not sleep well. Actually that is an understatement, he did not sleep at all. He lay in bed, his tired brain desperately trying to understand the change in events the previous evening. He began to wonder why Marston had not phoned him back. Eventually he convinced himself that wherever Marston had followed the car it could not have been important. It was a dangerous conviction.

In his thoughts he decided that Cavendish must have gone round to see Simon Derwent for some reason relating to his brother. Perhaps she wanted to patch things up after the furious row he had witnessed the evening before. Perhaps there was nothing to it after all. That had to be the case. And what about Sharon Mortimer? Well, she'd done as expected and taken the report and envelope round to Simon Derwent. Palmer wondered what the reaction would be when they opened the pictures. Probably not so big now they had something on video against Mortimer himself. But that was all just a relationship issue, nothing too serious. Actually everything balanced itself out quite nicely.

Probably she'd been surprised to see Cavendish, but as business partners Mortimer probably knew about Cavendish's fling with Richard Derwent. It all began to fit nicely into place. If Richard Derwent was right about the events a year before then he could provide Cavendish with her alibi – no problem. It was just beginning to all fit into place. Really, all the excitement of the previous evenings had been nothing more than that - excitement. All he hoped was Cavendish would square her row with Derwent and patch up that relationship. It would make it much easier when he was asked to give her the alibi.

The obvious questions eluded Palmer as his tired, over exercised brain sorted out its owner's problems. It all fitted extremely nicely. What had started out as being simple, had got unnecessarily complex, and had finally come to a nice, simple conclusion. He could tell Nash the same in the morning.

Slowly, very slowly, Palmer slipped into a state of unconsciousness. It was a troubled state of slumber that invaded his mind. It lasted until the first rays of the dawn sun filtered into his bedroom. It was not the weak arrival of light that awakened him, but the relatively loud clamour of the alarm clock that demanded his attention.

In a moment he turned over in his bed and silenced the clock that was invading his precious world of sleep. In another moment the events of the previous evening came flooding back and Palmer sat bolt upright.

"Could it be that simple?" His question was audible but there was no one to hear it. "Could it really be that simple? Could I have been so wrong?" As he rose from the bed, washed, shaved and dressed, Palmer kept asking himself the same question. "Could it be that simple?"

There was, he surmised, only one way to find out, and that was to see what happened at the offices of Goodland, Peasbody, and Nash, later that morning. Somewhere in the back of his mind, something still bothered him.

Palmer made himself busy. He breakfasted and took the camera out of his coat pocket. A few minutes later he was in his makeshift darkroom with the back off the camera. Even as the film developed in the darkness Palmer's mind was elsewhere. Then a question came to him.

"Exactly," he spoke out loud. "If Derwent can give her the alibi, why did she come to me? After all, she must have talked to him about it. Much simpler for him just to give it to her, rather than all this fuss."

The film developed, Palmer began the simple process of producing prints from the negatives. Haversham, he figured, would want prints. As they formed beneath his gaze, Palmer let out a low whistle. Marston was not wrong. These pictures were not what Palmer had expected. Maybe he had expected an affair, but the pictures of the two women were entirely unexpected. He had to admit, though, Marston's photographic efforts were quite good. Not so good, he imagined, as the pictures that had been taken in the bedroom itself. For a moment he wondered just what those pictures were for. Colin Haversham had seemed a reserved sort of person, and from his description of his wife she had similar leanings. Yet here she was, clearly visible, in all her naked splendour, and quite obviously not only enjoying herself but even, dare he think it, promoting her body in some way? Palmer was still musing over the snapshots of the activities when the phone rang. It was still not yet eight o'clock, but something about the ringing sound distracted

Palmer's admiration of the two females before him. He reached out a hand and picked up the telephone extension he had wisely installed in the darkroom.

"Damien, it's Eddie. How are you this morning?"

"Not too bad, but you didn't ring back. What happened."

"They drove off to a house south of Cheam. Big house called "The Laurels". It has got its own drive and gates and stuff. Anyway they didn't stay long, maybe five minutes. Then they left. They drove around a bit and then headed off down the A217 until they got south of Reigate. They pulled up at some flats and went inside. I waited an hour and then gave up and went home. It was late so I thought I'd phone you first thing. Not much to it, I suppose."

"No, guess not. I'm sure I've heard the name of that house before. What was it again?"

"The Laurels."

"Big house, was it, in an open country road? Not too many other houses?"

"That's it. Do you know it?"

"Should do. I've been there! That's Simon Derwent's brother's place. Remember he was the bloke who owned the house you watched yesterday. Wonder why they went there?"

"I have no idea. Couldn't see a thing with the fence. Actually I'd only just parked up when they came out again. Couldn't have been more than five minutes, probably less. Anyway, is there anything you need me for today?"

"Possibly. I've got to go and see Cavendish's solicitor at ten thirty. I'll let you know after that."

"Right, then, I'll go and do some shopping first off."

"Take your mobile, and leave it on. I'll contact you if I need you. I had a dream last night that we'd solved this and I'd given Cavendish her alibi, but something's nagging me. Anyway, I'll phone you later. Oh, one more thing."

"Yes?" Marston's voice was almost uninterested.

"Those pictures you took. They're pretty good, and pretty hot. Can you do a report to go with them? Might as well drop it off at Haversham's place later on."

"I've already E-Mailed you it. I couldn't sleep when I got back so I did it then."

"Great. I'll settle up with you later on. Talk to you then."

Palmer replaced the receiver and returned to the pictures. They were, indeed, hot stuff. Very revealing in fact. Palmer could not help but believe that the pictures taken in the room were promotional, but what for he could not tell. It did not bother him for long, as it was not his problem. That, if he wanted to, would be for Haversham to resolve.

The report from Marston was succinct and lacked detail. Palmer spent half an hour embellishing some of the details and preparing the invoice. At the end he placed the report, pictures, and invoice in a manila envelope and put the envelope in his battered, brown, briefcase.

The day had begun well, a case solved before nine o'clock in the morning! Palmer opened the post that had arrived while he was working. It took him only a few minutes to scan the various business requests. He would attend to them later on. For now, he had to contend with the Cavendish case. If he was fortunate it would all be resolved in a couple of hours and he would be able to get on with the rest of his work, if he was lucky.

The next hour passed slowly. Palmer deliberated the various options open to him. He considered the possibility of direct confrontation. That, he considered, would be unlikely to work. Cavendish would not want all and sundry to know about her nocturnal activities, and provided they did not materially affect the case, they were really none of his business either. Perhaps a more subtle approach would be needed. Perhaps he could use subtlety to get her to recall of her own free will the simple fact that she had been with Richard Derwent on the night of the accident and that he was her alibi. She could recall the meal and being with Derwent, but Palmer kept asking himself, why she could not accept the date of the meal, nor why she could not approach Derwent directly, especially as it was now obvious she still had a relationship with him. Palmer was puzzled. It had to be something significant about the date.

Suddenly, as he was puzzling over this final issue, he had an idea. He reached out and dragged the case folder out of his desk drawer. He fumbled through the various reports until he came to the coroner's report. He read it carefully as if looking for a vital piece of evidence, evidence that had been overlooked as insignificant. He read the report through twice, slowly. The only thing that sprang to mind was the almost inconsequential note that the car had been travelling in excess of 60 miles per hour, a speed that might have been considered somewhat high in view of the road conditions. It was not the cause of death, but it was a contributory factor.

The speed of the car had been high and there was no doubt about it. The skid marks had been carefully and correctly measured and the standard calculations performed. The question Palmer now raised in his mind was, why? Why was the car travelling so fast? Everything Palmer had learned about John Baker over the past few days indicated that he was a law-abiding, sensible, man who didn't take too many risks, and certainly not risks when driving. So why?

Logically, thought Palmer, the car was going fast, because it had been going fast. He remembered his own visit to the restaurant a few days earlier. He recalled the very corner where the BMW had crashed so tragically sixteen months earlier. He also remembered the long stretch of straight road leading up to the corner. Of course when he had travelled along it he had been going in the opposite direction to the BMW and had come out of the corner onto the straight. Coming from the other way, he now thought, he would have been travelling quite fast down the inviting straight stretch of road. He would have applied the brakes so as to get round the corner, and surely that is what Baker had done. The skid marks suggested he'd at least started to brake.

Then Palmer recalled his journey through Sutton a few days earlier. His brakes had failed when he'd been going along the one-way system. What if Baker's foot brake had failed? Instinctively, like Palmer, he would have used the handbrake. In Palmer's case it had stopped him several yards down the road. In Baker's case it had been too little, too late. Suddenly Palmer's eyes were wide open.

If that were the case then Baker hadn't died, he'd been murdered. If someone had tampered with his brakes, like Palmer had so recently experienced, then it was murder. But why would anyone do such a thing? And how could anyone be certain Baker would die just then, that evening? After all, Pete, his mechanic friend, had shown him how a small leak could take ages to take effect.

Baker had driven from home to the restaurant quite successfully. Clearly he had not been worried about the car's performance. If he had, as a cautious man, he would have called out the RAC or AA or some other organisation, Palmer continued in his mind.

Palmer had to admit that the brakes on the BWM could have been tampered with while Baker was in the restaurant, but that seemed unlikely. After all, the restaurant was busy and the car park well used. But, it was a possibility. Of course, after the crash, it had been impossible to determine whether the brakes were working at the time of the accident. One entire front wheel had been ripped off in the collision, and the other was so badly mangled that it was almost unrecognisable. That much was in the report.

Palmer continued to play with the thought that the brakes had been tampered with for a reason. The question he kept asking himself was what the reason could be? What was the motive? Why would anyone want John and Samantha Baker dead?

Palmer continued in this way for over an hour. Then, as if waking from a dream, he remembered the appointment with Nash. He felt even less convinced about it now than he had the previous evening as he had lain in bed.

Palmer arrived at the offices of Goodland, Peasbody, and Nash just as his watch showed the time to be ten thirty.

"Damien Palmer for Mr. Nash," Palmer spoke softly to the receptionist.

"One moment sir." She pressed a button on the console and spoke into the phone. "Mr. Palmer for you, sir." She replaced the receiver and looked at Palmer. "Mr. Nash will be right down. Do take a seat."

"Thank you," said Palmer softly. He had barely sat down when the tall, wiry, frame of Nash appeared in the doorway.

"Mr. Palmer, do come up."

Palmer followed the solicitor to his office.

"And the redoubtable Miss Cavendish, where is she?" Palmer began the conversation, when he saw that he and Nash were the sole occupants of the room.

"I have no idea," came the solicitor's reply. I talked to her yesterday afternoon, and she seemed quite happy with coming here this morning."

"Hmm. Well, I have a busy day, but I really do need to ask her a few questions. Thing is, I might have located her an alibi, but it is going to need a little bit of luck to make it work."

"How do you mean?"

"Well, someone I think she knows might have been with her on the evening in question. Only problem is, I don't know if that person would be willing to admit it. Anyway, we can find out when your client arrives. Any chance of a coffee, only I'm suffering from caffeine deficiency this morning."

"Of course, I should have offered it when you came in. So the case, as far as you can tell, is almost over?" The enquiry was genuine.

"Yes, I think so. A few loose ends, and some unanswered questions."

"Such as?"

"Well, for instance, why did your partner David Goodland get killed?"

"Well, that surely isn't anything to do with this case. Or do you think it is?"

"To be honest, I don't know. Probably, like you said, but it's a pretty gruesome coincidence. I take the police haven't given you any more information."

"Only that he died from a broken neck, probably as a result from falling off the cliffs into the water. Bound to have hit a rock or something."

"Hmm. There is another train of thought I've been pursuing, but I can't for the life of me think why anyone would go to the extent of killing someone, especially not Goodland."

"Well, as we have no client, you could expand if you wanted." Nash's offer was, thought Palmer, a little too generous.

"Well, for example. Could he have ruffled anyone's feathers through his job? Rhetorical, I think not. Okay, people don't always get along with you guys, but that isn't a motive for murder, is it? So, I had this wild thought that there might be something in his past. Perhaps before you knew him?"

"I doubt it. We went to university together. Had some good times too, I can tell you, so I guess I've always known David. Okay, he was a bit wild at University, but who isn't, and anyway that was several years ago now. I really don't think there's anyone I know who'd want David dead, it's just not possible."

"Well, it was only a theory. I didn't know you'd known him that long."

"Yes. Anyway, where is this woman? I have other clients to attend to?"

"Quite so, and I have a busy day too? Tell me, though, at university…"

"Yes, what?" Nash was clearly becoming impatient at the tardiness of his client.

"At university, did Goodland ever get into any real trouble?"

"As I said before, no he didn't. We weren't exactly social partners, and he was always a bit of a womaniser. But no, I'm not aware of anything."

"And those women friends. One of them wasn't called Samantha by any chance, was she?"

"Samantha? Let me think. There might have been, briefly. It's a few years back now. Why?"

"Well, how about Samantha Collins?"

"Yes, come to think of it there was someone with a name like that. But it was only a fleeting relationship. Lasted maybe a couple of weeks. But now you mention it, there was a Sam Collins in the Hall. She was quite attractive too, if I remember rightly. But it was years ago. How did you come across her?"

"Just doing my job. A bit of detection and some guesswork actually. Well, I don't think I need to stay here any longer. Your client won't be coming here today."

"And how are you suddenly so sure?"

"Because she knows who you are, and if I were you I would not go out today, at least not until I call you. You could be in the gravest of danger. Now, I must act quickly before anybody else gets hurt."

"But what's it to do with me? And why am I in danger? And shouldn't you tell the police?"

"Okay, first question first, and then I must go. Cast your mind back to university, to one particular evening when you, Goodland, and a few others had a lot to drink and a certain woman ended up in a van with you." Nash went pale at the thought.

"Remember?" Palmer had stopped playing games.

"Yes," he replied weakly.

"And who was the woman?"

"Sam Collins, and she was drunk too."

"I haven't got time for excuses. You all took turns, and since then she's been getting even with you, hasn't she?"

"Yes. How do you know all this?"

"I ask a lot of questions. Now, two of your friends have already been publicly humiliated, haven't they? Goodland was the third, and I'm guessing you're the fourth. So that means you are in danger."

"So, what do I do?"

"You stay here while I find Cavendish?"

"But what's she got to do with it, her first name isn't Sam, it's Helen."

"I know, and believe me I'd love to sit here and explain everything, but there isn't time. I have to get on or other people will get hurt. Now, one final thing, if Cavendish does turn up then my guesswork has been wrong. If she does, don't tell her anything, and above all, don't let her go."

"Fair enough." A little of Nash's colour had returned to his cheeks.

With that, Palmer stood up and left the office. He returned to his car and with a good degree of haste set off for his next destination, a flat in Wimbledon.

The roads were mercifully not particularly busy and in less than half an hour Palmer was standing outside the block of flats where he had finished up the previous evening. As he drove there this morning his mind was working overtime. He knew that he had to get back inside the flat. As he stood there now, his hand tapped the diary in his coat pocket. He'd carefully wiped it of his prints, and now he needed to return it. He tapped his other pocket and located the two keys he had been prudent enough to hold onto, despite the assurances he'd given to the contrary. There was only one more obstacle – the entry phone system. He still regretted the fact that he had not obtained the combination from Cavendish when he'd had the chance.

He made his way up the pathway to the front of the flats. He pressed the button for the doorbell for flat seven. He knew that there would be no response. The light coloured Fiesta was no longer parked where it had been left the previous evening. Palmer held the mobile phone to his ear, waiting for a response.

"Eddie, you took your time."

"Sorry, Damien, I was in traffic."

"Where are you?"

"Nearly home, why?"

"Well, I don't know for sure, but Cavendish looks like she's done a runner. Could you drop your stuff off and get on the road towards Sutton, or actually get back to the house from last night."

"Sure thing, but what am I looking for?"

"Nothing yet, but I think she's coming back that way."

"Okay. I'll be about five minutes and then I'll be on my way. Take a good forty minutes to get there though."

"Yeah I know. I'll join you when I've finished here. Talk to you later." Palmer finished the call and put the phone back into his pocket.

Then he turned his attention to the front door of the flats. He need not have worried for one of the occupants of the ground floor was coming towards him.

"It's all right. Someone's just coming out," he called out, as if talking into the intercom. As he did so the door opened and the elderly gentleman exited the building. "Just saved her from pressing the doorbell," said Palmer jovially as he held the door open. The elderly gentleman muttered something and continued on his way.

In a minute Palmer was standing outside flat seven. In another minute he had gained entry to the flat. His first task was to replace the diary. He'd long since photographed the relevant page and the diary now needed to be returned to its rightful place. Carefully he took the diary out of his pocket. It was wrapped in a plastic envelope and he was careful not to touch it as he put it back on the bookshelf. It would have looked peculiar to put it back in the sofa, so Palmer decided to replace it on the bookshelf.

That accomplished, he took a quick look round. It was soon clear that the woman had packed a case. A number of her clothes were missing, as were a couple of cases. This was not surprising to Palmer. Indeed he would have been more surprised had the clothes been present.

He went into the bathroom. To one side was a wicker laundry basket. Palmer, using the edge of one finger pushed the lid upwards. The basket was almost empty, but at the bottom, screwed up in a ball was what he was looking for. The pale brown cardigan that Cavendish had been wearing the previous evening was waiting for someone to find it. On it was a dark red brown patch. Palmer looked at it cautiously, not wanting to pick it up. His experience told him not to touch what would undoubtedly be evidence. There was no mistaking it. His assertion of the previous evening was right. This was blood. With great care he lowered the lid of the laundry basket. He made one further, careful, examination of the flat and then left. There was nothing more of interest.

Palmer returned to his car and began his own journey to Sutton. With Marston already on his way to the house in Worcester Park there was no point in Palmer going there. As he drove he remembered the manila envelope in his briefcase. As he did so he turned off the main road in Wimbledon Village and headed off towards the opulent area of the park. He found the Haversham's house and stopped. The white Peugeot was nowhere to be seen. To be sure Palmer picked up the mobile phone and dialled a number.

"Hello," came the response a few seconds later.

"Colin Haversham?" Palmer's tone of voice was questioning.

"Yes, who's speaking?"

"Sorry to trouble you, it's Damien Palmer. Can you talk?"

"Yes, I'm quite alone."

"In which case, do you mind if I come in. I'm parked just up the road. Only I had to check first."

"Sure, but she'll be back in half an hour."

"That's fine. I only have a few minutes, but I was in the area so I thought I'd give it a try." Palmer was now walking towards the front door of the Haversham house. He'd just reached the door when the man inside opened it.

"Right, we don't need this anymore."

"Come in, please. Take a seat."

Palmer hated these moments. The anxious client waiting for news, and Palmer having to work out how best to approach what was always a sensitive issue.

"You have some news then?" Haversham continued nervously.

"Yes. But it's not what you are thinking. There is definitely no other man involved."

"Well, that's a relief anyway. So what did she get up to yesterday evening?"

"I think you'd better sit down and have a look at this. It contains the agent's reports and some photographs. It's probably best if you draw your own conclusions. Oh, and I have included our fee note, which I'd be grateful if you could settle in the next week or so."

"You can have a cheque now if you want?"

"That would be helpful, but perhaps you should take a look at the report first."

Palmer handed the manila envelope over to Haversham who opened it nervously. It so happened that he extracted the invoice first. He looked at it for no more than three seconds.

"Very reasonable, I would have expected more. I can settle that today."

Then he pulled out the report and the array of photographs. He looked at them for a moment and went white. He read the report again, and looked over the pictures.

"So what the hell is she doing?"

"I really don't know. It could be a number of things, but my guess, if you want one, is that she's doing some shots for a magazine or something, and then she's just mucking around afterwards."

"Hmm. Where are the negatives?"

"In the envelope, and there is only one set of prints. It is entirely up to you what you do with them next."

"Confront her with them of course."

"Is that the best idea? You have the address, so you no longer need to follow her. Perhaps it would be better to just turn up there next time she goes there. That way it won't look like you've paid someone to snoop on her."

"You may be right. But this stuff is disgusting."

"Yes, I thought you'd be offended."

"Yes, anyway, Mr. Palmer, thank you for your efforts. Now, my cheque book, where is it?" Haversham returned the report and pictures to the envelope that he then took out of the lounge where they were sitting. In a minute he returned with a neatly written cheque in his hand.

"I think that covers it, and once again, many thanks. If I need your services further I take it you will be happy to oblige?" His voice had regained a degree of composure though his face was still ashen.

"Of course, and thank you for this." Palmer pocketed the cheque. "Now I must be on my way, and good luck, however you decide to approach things."

Palmer made his way to the door and then to his car. Once inside the vehicle he paused for a moment and rubbed the back of his neck. There was a tension in his body that came with the suspense of anticipated action. It often affected him this way. For a fleeting moment he thought of his forthcoming appointment at the Beauty Centre in Sutton and he imagined the expert fingers of Sharon Mortimer working the tension out of his body. It was a pleasing thought and helped him to relax a bit. After a minute it was time to resume his journey in the direction of Sutton.

For this next phase in the Cavendish case Palmer didn't really have a game plan. He knew where she was not, but he had no idea where he might find her. He picked up the mobile phone and pressed some buttons.

"Eddie," he began, when he got a response. "Where are you?"

"I've just pulled up outside the house. Everything seems quiet here."

"It won't be for long. Listen to me carefully. I've just been to Cavendish's flat. She's done a runner. Taken some clothes and bags. More importantly she's left a cardigan in the laundry basket that's covered in blood."

"Delightful."

"Yeah. Now either she's getting careless, or she's basically saying she isn't intending to come back."

"Or she doesn't think we're onto her?" Marston's query was purely conversational.

"Not a chance of that, I'm afraid. The report and pictures weren't in her flat, and I doubt they're still where you are, so I'm going over to the other Derwent house to take a look."

"What do you want me to do?"

"I think it's best if you just stay where you are for now. I don't like the look of all that blood on her cardigan. I think it's time someone with authority took a look in that place. I want you to tell me what happens. Okay?" Palmer's question was out of deference to the fact that he knew Marston hated any contact with authority, especially the authority he had in mind.

"Guess so. How long?"

"Don't know. I'll put the call through now. So about ten minutes I should think."

"Okay. I'll call you later."

"Cheers Eddie." Palmer ended the call and dialled 999. Leaving a short message and without giving his own details away he suggested a crime was taking place at the house Marston was watching. It would suffice for now, and he could square the record later, but he needed to find Cavendish as soon as possible. The call ended, Palmer continued on his journey to Sutton and the country beyond. He knew it would take at least twenty minutes to drive to Richard Derwent's country residence.

Back in Worcester Park events happened very swiftly indeed. Marston had parked behind the children's playground and waited. Palmer's estimate of ten minutes proved to be conservative. Marston had checked the clock and noted five minutes had elapsed when the Panda car arrived. Two police constables alighted and went and knocked on the door. There was, of course, no response. The curtains in the front room were still drawn so Marston saw one of the constables push open the letterbox and peer in.

Marston judged that whatever the constable saw must have been of considerable interest to him for in less than ten seconds he and his colleague were using their shoulders to break down the front door. It took them only a few attempts before the door gave way. Then all went quiet again.

There was a small group of children playing on the swings and slides. They carried on, oblivious of the drama unfolding across the road. Their mothers, having initially observed the police car arriving, had now continued with their conversation. Indeed they were so engrossed that they failed to notice the policeman who approached them, until he coughed gently. Marston had the window of the passenger door down.

"Err, excuse me madam."

The women looked up and were immediately surprised.

"Yes, officer," one of them said.

"Are you from round here."

"Yes. Live over the back there." She pointed vaguely over in Marston's direction. "Why?"

"Well, there's been an incident. I don't suppose you've heard or seen anything unusual today, have you?"

"No. What kind of incident?"

"I'm sorry, madam. I can't say. But you might like to take the kiddies off home now. We'll have to close the park and probably the area around it too."

The women started to gather their things and called their children back from where they were happily playing.

"And before you go I need to have your names and addresses. Someone may want to speak to you later."

The women obliged and then, having collected their offspring, they made their way out of the park. As they did so, three more police cars, an ambulance, and an incident van screamed up the road to stop outside the house. The next thing Marston could see was a constable sealing off an area around the front of the house with the usual blue and white striped tape. That done he came over and tied some more tape to the gate that led into the playground. Marston decided that he'd seen enough.

Palmer had just pulled up in the gateway some one hundred metres away from Derwent's country house when the mobile phone rang.

"Eddie, how's it going?"

"Bleeding awful. There's something bad gone on in that house. The pigs have sealed the house off, quite a bit of pavement and the kids" park. Now four cop cars are standing out the front, an ambulance, and an incident van. No doubt a posse of reporters will be here soon."

"I shouldn't think so, unless you want there to be."

"No I don't. Anyway, there must be half a dozen people gone in the house by now, including a couple of paramedics. What the fuck's going on Damien?" His voice carried a definite air of agitation, the tone of which was not lost on Palmer.

"Well, I don't know for sure. But I'm guessing they're going to find a body in there. Now, do you feel okay to stay for a bit?"

"Hang on, something's happening. The medic guys have just come out. They don't look too happy. Wait a moment." Palmer waited. "Yeah, they've got in the ambulance and killed the lights. Yeah, they're driving off."

"Shit," Palmer whispered, barely audibly.

"What was that?"

"I just said shit."

"Oh. Any reason?"

"No, it was just something to say. Anything else happening?"

"Nope. The cops are still inside, and there's a bobby on the door now. I'd guess they've found someone inside. What do you want me to do?"

"Hang on a bit, I think. I've just pulled up at Derwent's. Give me five minutes to check it out and I'll get back to you."

"Okay."

Palmer ended the call and alighted from his car. He walked the hundred metres to Derwent's drive and slowed down as he approached the gateway. Peering round the hedge he noticed the light coloured Fiesta parked in the driveway. There was no sign of Derwent's own vehicle. Palmer cautiously made his way to the front of the Fiesta and felt the bonnet. It was cold.

"Damn," he swore softly to himself, "been here for ages."

He approached the house and peered in through the windows. There was no sign of life, not even the Doberman.

For good measure Palmer pressed the doorbell before running back down the drive. He waited at the entrance to the drive to see what happened, but his wait was in vain. There very clearly wasn't anyone at home. After a couple of minutes he made his way back to the Fiesta and made a more thorough examination. The car was locked but Palmer could see what looked like bloodstains on both the mat on the driver's side and also on the driver's seat. Other than the stains there was little of interest.

Palmer heard the sound of a vehicle coming up the road. He was still looking through the window of the Fiesta when something told him the vehicle was changing down through the gears. His mind was still preoccupied with the Fiesta when he heard the car stop and one of the doors being slammed shut. Then he heard the sound of footsteps on the gravel drive. The sound was coming from his right and it was getting nearer. Palmer dropped down behind the passenger side of the car and inched his way forward. He could hear the steps now, each one getting louder and louder. Then quite suddenly the steps stopped. Palmer judged the owner of the feet was standing directly the other side of the car.

Then Palmer heard the car door being opened. In seconds the door was slammed shut and the occupier of the car started the engine. Palmer crouched low, waiting for the moment of discovery. As the engine started, the car in the road pulled away. Palmer caught a brief glimpse of a small, dark, car as it passed the driveway. Now the Fiesta was on the move. Slowly at first, but gathering pace as the driver steered the vehicle out of the drive.

Palmer paced the car to begin with until he came to the large rhododendron bush. As he did so he judged the moment and with a violent thrust, forced himself away from the car. He rolled over into the bush and lay still for several seconds, waiting for the driver of the car to stop and come after him. The Fiesta carried on. The driver reached the end of the drive and turned left, following the car that had just pulled away in the road.

As he rolled away Palmer caught a glimpse of the driver. He could not be sure, but there was a certain familiarity in what he saw.

It took Palmer a few seconds to react. As he did so, he picked his phone out of his pocket. He pressed some buttons, and waited.

"Alan Brown," the voice was deep.

"Alan, hi, it's Damien Palmer, long time no see. How are you?"

"I'm on duty actually. Can I call you back later? I didn't recognise your number."

"I changed it a few months ago. No, I need to talk now. It's important."

Palmer went on to explain why it was important. He explained, as quickly as he could, why the head of security at Gatwick airport should be called from a mobile phone while he was on duty, and what the significance of the call was.

"You realise that she could be using any name, don't you," Brown said eventually.

"Yeah, I know, but I don't think she is. It'll be one of those, and my guess is she's picking up the ticket at your end, if she hasn't done so already. Any chance you could help?"

"Well, it's strictly out of order, but I guess it wouldn't hurt. Look, I'll get onto the ticket booths and see if we turn up anything. Are you sure she's headed this way?"

"No. It could be Heathrow, or Luton. But I have a hunch it's Gatwick. Alan if you locate her, she may have a friend with her. It's vital they're both apprehended. Use whatever pretext you like, but keep them there please. I'll be there in about half an hour. Also, I want a chat with her before the police do. I know things that could save some lives if I can get her to co-operate."

"Well, it's a big favour to ask." Brown sounded less than convinced.

"I know, but you're the only one I can ask. So what about it?"

"Okay, I'll take a look. You owe me one, Damien."

"Yeah, and cheers."

Palmer pressed some more buttons on the phone and waited for the phone on the other end to ring.

"John Nash, please. It's urgent and personal."

He waited no more than five seconds before being put through.

"John, it's Damien Palmer. I don't have much time, but I'm pretty sure your client is about to flee the country. Can you meet me at the entrance to the departure lounge at Gatwick in forty minutes? I thought you'd want to be there when she's questioned."

"I can't possibly be there. I have a client in ten minutes."

"John, this is really important. Your client has probably killed at least two people in the last twenty-four hours and there may be others. I need you there when I talk to her for the sake of propriety, but if you're not there I'll have to talk to her any way. There are lives at stake here."

"Okay, okay. I'll be there. Departure lounge entrance, you said?" His voice sounded exasperated.

"Yeah. Do you know where it is?"

"Through the check in desks, in the middle somewhere isn't it?"

"That's it. If I'm not there, someone will meet up with you. Must go." Palmer didn't bother to explain his last statement. Even as he was speaking he had begun running back to his own car.

Acting on his hunch Palmer swung the car out onto the road and with a degree of haste that was not entirely suitable to the road he headed south. It took him just over half an hour to reach the turn off on the M23 that led to the North and South termini at Gatwick. As he reached the turn off he remembered the two termini and also that he had no idea which one she would be heading for. He picked the South out of habit. It was familiar territory to him and he knew the layout well. He had just parked on the third level of car park 2 when the mobile rang.

"Palmer," he spoke hastily,

"Damien, it's Alan Brown. She has a ticket ordered from the BA desk in the South Terminal. It's not been collected yet."

"Great. Where is she going to?"

"Palma. Not exactly exotic, but it is becoming more of a gateway these days."

"Yeah. Innocuous way out of England and then she disappears. That's clever, very clever. Look, thanks for that. I'm on the third floor of car park 2. Can I meet you at the BA desk in say five minutes?"

"Yeah. I'll just hang around. But what if she turns up, won't she recognise you?"

"Yeah, but I have to get to her as quickly as possible. There's probably a couple of people who are already dead, and a few more that are in real danger."

"You sure?"

"Fairly sure, but some of it is guess work for now. See you in a minute."

Palmer turned off the mobile phone and exited his car. Two minutes later he arrived at the entrance of the check-in area of the South Terminal. He'd barely walked off the horizontal escalator when a man in a security guard's uniform approached him.

"Alan, good to see you." Palmer reached out a hand of welcome.

"Damien. There's still no sign of the target. Her ticket is still unclaimed. What next?"

"We wait. When's the flight?"

"It's due to leave in just over hour and a half. She should be checking in by now really."

"Yeah. She'll be late. I guess she's got some loose ends to tie up first. Damn, can we go to your office? I need to make a few calls."

"Sure, it's just up those stairs. Do you want me to wait here?"

"No. Presumably we can monitor this area from up there?"

"Of course."

"Well, let's go then."

In a couple of minutes Palmer was sitting in the office of the head of airport security. In front of him a bank of screens showed pictures from various parts of the airport complex. As he sat down, Brown pressed some buttons on a console and the central, large, screen changed to show a view of the BA ticket desk in the check-in area. Palmer pulled the mobile phone out of his jacket pocket and called a number.

"Eddie," he began, "what's happening?"

"Loads. There's a coroner's van outside the house now and a couple of minutes ago they brought out something on a stretcher. Haven't driven off yet. Where are … hang on, something's happening."

Palmer waited patiently for his colleague to continue.

"Another stretcher's coming out. They've got the rear door of the van open again and they're sliding it in. There's still about half a dozen cop cars here and there's a group of people standing around the taped off area. Where are you?"

"Gatwick. Right, you're finished there. I need you to get down here as quickly as possible. You know the turn off the M23, the roundabout. Well, I need you to pull over on the roundabout and watch for a vehicle. It's a four-wheel drive, dark blue. If you spot it, then follow it." Palmer continued to read out the registration of the vehicle.

"Why the roundabout?" Marston was curious.

"Because I reckon it's in one of the car parks here and it would take all day to find it. If it leaves the chances are it will come past the roundabout. How long will it take you to get there?"

"About an hour I should think. They're driving the van off now. Anything else?"

"Not for now but I'll ring you if anything changes."

"Okay. And what are you going to do?"

"Wait here and hope she turns up. Talk to you later."

Palmer switched off the phone and turned his attention to the screen. The minutes ticked slowly by. Passengers walked past the screen and a few even stopped at the BA ticket desk. The minutes turned into a half hour. Then, just as Palmer was beginning to wonder whether his feelings had been right a familiar figure appeared. Richard Derwent, suddenly appeared from the direction of the car parks and walked up to the BA ticket desk.

"That's the boyfriend." Palmer pointed to the screen as he talked.

"Well, where is she?"

"Why?"

"Well, she has to personally claim her ticket. He can't collect it for her. Security regulations."

Palmer sat and reflected on this piece of news. Derwent had handed over his credit card and was waiting for the transaction to be authorised.

"And you checked on the name Derwent?"

"Yeah. Nothing."

"So what's he picking up then?" Palmer looked concerned.

Before he had even finished the sentence Alan Brown was on the phone. He spoke softly but with authority. When he put the phone down he turned to Palmer.

"Credit card id a company one, in the name of Baker and Derwent, and the ticket is in the name of Baker. Are you sure that's your man."

"Positive," said Palmer, and smiled. "And now, it makes perfect sense. Incidentally, is the ticket for a Mr. or Mrs. Baker?"

"Didn't say I'm afraid. Do you want me to check?"

"No. There's no need to."

As he spoke he remembered the words his lover, Karen Shaw, had spoken on the way back from the restaurant a few nights previously. Her feeling had indeed proved to be right.

"We have to follow him, and find out where Cavendish is. He's not going anywhere without her, and she's here somewhere."

"Unless they are travelling separately, after all there was only one ticket in the name of Baker."

"Could be, but she's here somewhere."

The man at the BA ticket desk was putting his credit card away. As he completed this task he picked up the ticket that lay on the tabletop and walked away. Silently the surveillance camera followed him. It followed him to the entrance to the car parks.

"Quick," said Palmer in a voice that suggested he now understood everything. "She's in the car park. The fool left her there while he came and paid for the ticket. We've got to find her."

"Why?"

"Simple. Up to now she has covered her treacherous tracks with a path of death. You hardly think she's going to leave the one person who knows who and where she is alive do you? We've got to stop her, and him."

Palmer was already opening the office door as he spoke. In his hand the mobile phone was already dialling the number he required.

"Eddie?"

"Yeah."

"Where are you?"

"I'm on the M23, with about four miles to go. Traffic's not bad so I should be there in five minutes. Why?"

"Because I think he is about to leave. If so it could be tight. Can you step on it a bit?"

"Not really, and anyway I've been thinking. If he's got a four-wheel drive I'm going to find it hard to follow him if he takes off."

Whilst they were talking Palmer had run to the exit to the car parks. Derwent, predictably, had disappeared.

"Damn it," Palmer continued almost to himself.

"What?" Marston's query broke through into Palmer's concentration.

"Just that I've lost him. He could be anywhere."

"Two more miles to go, I'll have to hang up now. I need to concentrate on the traffic."

"Cheers Eddie."

Palmer switched off the phone and looked up. The head of security was at his side.

"What next?" He queried.

"Dunno. But I still think the woman is here somewhere." At that moment as Palmer looked down the corridor to the car parks, he spotted the woman walking towards him.

"That's her." Palmer sounded not quite triumphant.

"Sure?"

"Oh yeah. Now we need to have her stopped."

Palmer had turned his back on the direction from which the woman was walking. He judged the moment and spun round. The woman was not more than four feet from him. Her surprise was complete as Palmer spoke.

"Miss Cavendish, could we have a word please?"

The head of security had taken up position behind the woman, cutting off any hope of escape.

Helen Cavendish pursed her lips and stood frozen to the spot.

"Now Miss Cavendish, where exactly is Mr. Derwent?"

Cavendish pursed her lips harder and refused to talk.

"Do I take it that he has left you here and taken the car away?"

"Yeah. And in about five minutes he'll go the same way as his brother, and there's nothing you can do about it."

This outburst was not expected and it took Palmer a full five seconds to react. He did so by picking up the mobile phone and calling Marston.

"Eddie, the car's coming your way. Now listen very carefully. You have got to stop it, and in the next few minutes. We've apprehended Cavendish but I think she's planted something in the car. So don't get too close."

Palmer replaced the mobile phone and turned to his client. As he did so, two female security personnel arrived. The entourage steered Cavendish towards an interview room.

"There's just one more thing Miss Cavendish. I have found your alibi."

Back on the roundabout Marston had turned on the hazard lights. He'd pulled as far over on the roundabout as possible and turned off the engine. It was an old trick and he hoped desperately that the police would not trouble him. He need not have worried for in less than a couple of minutes he saw the blue vehicle coming towards him. He started the engine and turned off the hazard lights, though he waited until the vehicle had entered the roundabout before moving off. Fortunately the traffic was light and Marston was able to tuck in behind the target as they turned back onto the M23, heading North.

They gathered speed until they reached the magic 70 miles per hour. Marston struggled to keep pace initially. When he was sure that the vehicle was the right one he began to flash his headlights. With sweat pouring of his head he frantically waved to the driver ahead of him to pull over, though his efforts were in vain. Finally he pushed the accelerator to the floorboard and pulled out into the centre lane. He pulled up level with the blue vehicle and sounded his horn. Having attracted the attention of the driver he signalled for the driver to pull onto the hard shoulder. He looked at his watch. According to Palmer's earlier comments time had just run out. For a moment the blue vehicle continued on its course then, as Marston signalled even more frantically the driver pulled over.

Back at the airport five minutes passed. Cavendish sat sullenly on one side of the desk in the interview room. On the other side Palmer waited patiently. There was a knock at the door and the woman's solicitor entered. John Nash acknowledged Palmer and then asked for a few minutes alone with his client. Palmer saw no reason to complain and obligingly left the room along with the female security guard and Alan Brown. As he left the room his mobile phone sounded.

"Palmer."

"Damien, it's Eddie. I've got him onto the hard shoulder and convinced him to get out of his vehicle. What next?"

"Get the hell away from it. The police have been contacted and will be with you in a couple of minutes." As Palmer spoke, over the airwaves he heard the sound of what seemed like a deep-throated roar followed by a bang. It left him stunned. The sound of the bang echoed around the corridor, the security guard next to Palmer visibly shaken by the ferocity and intensity of the sound.

"Eddie, you still there?" Palmer's voice was choked, almost a whisper. He was greeted by static. After a few seconds he repeated the question. Again there was just static by way of response. On his third request he breathed a sigh of relief as his colleague replied.

"Yeah. Christ that was some explosion. We're going to need a fire engine as well now."

"Are either of you hurt?"

"No. Fuck that was one hell of a bang."

"Where's Derwent?"

"Beside me, and he's gone a paler shade of white than I've ever seen anyone go before."

"Put him on." Palmer waited as the telephone was handed over. "Mr. Derwent?"

"Err, yes. Who are you?"

"Damien Palmer, I'm a private investigator. Do you know anyone who might want to blow you up?"

"No."

"What about Sam Baker?"

"But, but, she's dead."

"No she isn't. She's sitting in an office not twenty feet from where I am. The pretence is over, Mr. Derwent. I imagine the police will want to question you about why your car exploded on the M23. That's for them. You might also wish to consider why. Also, you may wish to consider if there is anybody else who Sam Baker has a grudge against." Palmer heard the wailing sound of the police sirens over the phone. "Hand me back to Eddie." Again there was a pause as the phone was transferred.

"Eddie. Make sure he's taken into custody. You'll have to make a statement as well, though

I've already covered most of it. Say we meet at the Anchor at eight this evening?"

"Yeah. Anyway, the pigs are here now so I'll have to go." The phone went dead.

Alan Brown was standing next to Palmer.

"Her brief is sure taking his time." The comment was innocuous enough but for some reason it sent the sound of a claxon being fired through Palmer's brain. "Christ, did anybody search her before we left them alone." It was a general question and Palmer looked round at the people standing there as one by one they shook their heads. "Oh shit."

"We don't have that kind of power for something like this. We're almost breaking the rules as it is."

"Quick. You've got to interrupt them, she's got something on her brief."

Even as Palmer spoke urgently to the head of security he knocked politely on the door of interview room one. There was no response. He knocked louder. Still there was no answer. Palmer was now standing by the door. He turned the handle and pushed. The door was locked from the inside.

"Damn. We have to get that door open, and fast." Brown picked up his own pager and fired off a message. "And while you're at it you'd better get a paramedic down here. I think we're going to need one. Damn it." Palmer was sounding more frustrated than he had been all day. It riled him that his adversary had been smarter than he had cared to consider possible.

In less than two minutes another uniformed security guard arrived. It took him just five seconds to unlock the door. Palmer turned the handle and pushed the door open. Nash was sprawled across the table, head down. The white shirt, so immaculately clean earlier that day was now showing signs of blood, blood that was soaking into the shirt from whatever wound had been inflicted on him, a wound as yet masked by the table. It took Palmer two strides to reach the solicitor. He saw the growing pool of blood on the table and realised the wound was severe. He took his wrist and found a feint but regular pulse.

"He's still alive, just. Where's that bloody medic?"

As if in answer a green suited paramedic appeared in the doorway.

"All right sir, we'll take over now if you don't mind." The second paramedic arrived and together they began to work on the crumpled form of Nash. The room seemed crowded. For some reason all the security personnel had felt it necessary to crowd into the room. Palmer took a quick look round. It was obvious that Cavendish was no longer in the room.

"Alan, is there any other way out?" Palmer's question seemed futile. The room was an internal room with no windows and only artificial light. The only door was the one they had taken precious moments to break in through.

"None that I can think of, unless she did something crazy like crawled through the air conditioning duct. Now, anyone not directly involved in this, can you please get out of the room? We need to give the medics some space."

As Alan Brown made his request his command was immediately obeyed, and in less than thirty seconds only Palmer, Brown, the paramedics and their patient remained.

"This is turning into a nightmare," Brown commented as Palmer looked up at the grille covering the air conditioning duct.

"That's where she went. Look, the grille hasn't been refitted properly. God knows how she did it."

"Desperate people and all that."

"Oh, she's not desperate. I'll bet that even now she's back at the BA ticket desk buying her ticket out of this country. We have got to find her."

"You guys okay?" Brown questioned the paramedics, even as he punched a number into his pager.

"Yeah, have him out in a couple of minutes. It looks bad but there's only one puncture and lucky for him it doesn't look like it hit anything too vital. We'll take him to Crawley."

"Right, I'll get someone to go with him." Brown went out of the room and talked to one of the security guards that were still standing there.

"Now, Miss Cavendish, where have you gone?" Palmer asked the question rhetorically. "Let's see. We know you were in here and you went up the duct." Brown re-entered the room. "Where do the ducts go?"

"Just to the four interview rooms and then there's a long vertical column that leads to the main system. No way could she climb that."

"Don't bet on it. But for now, let's assume she went to one of the other interview rooms. Which one?"

"If it was me I'd go to number four. It's on the corner, so it's the easiest one to slip out of and disappear from."

"I agree." Palmer was already running out of the room and ran down the short corridor to interview room four. Unceremoniously he pushed the door open and looked in. The grille was lying on the floor, broken from its mountings.

"Well, that's what she did, and I'll bet she just walked out when we all rushed into the other room. A gamble, but it worked for her. Now to stop her getting that ticket."

"Too late I'm afraid. I phoned the desk a moment ago. She's already collected it. But don't worry. We'll get her when she goes through passport control. I've radioed through a special alert, and she hasn't had time to get through yet. We might as well go and wait for her there. She's only got fifteen minutes to being called for her flight so she can't leave it too much longer."

As he spoke, Brown and Palmer began their walk through the maze of corridors until they reached the central part of the whole departure procedure, the security checks and passport control. They waited behind the screen that afforded them some protection against recognition until it was too late. Sure enough, after ten minutes their efforts were rewarded. Cavendish flashed her red passport in the face of the security officer. Normally, for passengers travelling to other European countries that form part of the EEC this is a formality, and these days the security officers show scant regard for any European based passport. Cavendish breathed a sigh of relief too soon. Clearly the security officer was not convinced and he pointed to her to stop. She did so and waited while the officer took a closer look at her passport. She breathed again as he waved her through. As he did so, his left hand slid under the desk and he pressed the little red warning button. It flashed in the screened off area.

In less than ten seconds it was all over. Four armed security personnel appeared as if from nowhere and steered Cavendish behind the innocuous screen.

"Bastard," she spat at Palmer as she saw the smile on his face.

"I'm sorry Miss Cavendish, if that's what your passport says. But dead people don't usually travel abroad."

Chapter 10

That evening the Anchor pub was virtually empty. Around a small round table sat three people, locked in conversation. Palmer had bought the first round of drinks, if only because it was the least he could do for his friends. Eddie Marston looked pale. The explosion had obviously shaken him, and even with Palmer's lengthy account of events having been despatched to the police, Marston had still incurred a lengthy interrogation. Richard Derwent, equally shaken by the explosion was in custody. The charges would follow in the next few days. Likewise, the woman who had been with Derwent at Gatwick was under arrest. Sharon Mortimer, David Goodland and Simon Derwent were all dead. It had turned out to be a messy business. There was no denying it.

The two men each took a long swig of beer. Their companion, Karen Shaw, also sipped her lager.

"So, Damien, how did you work it out?" She asked the question after a few minutes.

"In the end it wasn't actually that difficult. I just wish I'd been a bit quicker off the mark. Might have saved Sharon Mortimer or Simon Derwent. We'll never know."

"So exactly how did you unravel this one?" Marston looked up from the beer. He was tired but intrigued.

"Well, it all began about four years ago. There was a successful architect called Robert Mortimer.

He was married to Sharon Mortimer and she was greedy. She had no real skills of her own, except that she was a damned good masseuse. I can vouch for that personally. Ouch!" The accurately aimed kick under the table was from the woman sitting opposite him. "She did my face, all right?"

"If you say so dear," Karen smiled.

"Well, there was another firm of architects called Baker and Derwent. Now John Baker had been to university with Robert Mortimer and knew how good he was. He also realised, too late in his career that he had teamed up with a greedy no-hoper in Richard Derwent. What Baker didn't know was just how greedy Derwent was. Sometime in the last few years Derwent had started an affair with his partner's wife, Sam, and discovered that she had contacts. I don't think Baker ever realised his wife was being unfaithful.

Not least of these contacts were her cousin Helen Cavendish. Now, it may surprise you, but Cavendish was a wealthy woman, or at least she used to be. Anyway Derwent had a younger brother, also a no-hoper, called Simon, only Simon was into drugs and things and he built up a list of creditors as long as your arm. Eventually they began to bay for blood.

Richard Derwent suggested to his brother that he was in the market to buy information from competitors. And so it happened that one day Simon Derwent walked into The Beauty Centre. It wasn't an accident. His brother had already told him that Cavendish owned it. Actually it was virtually all of Cavendish's money that went into starting up the business. She'd only met Sharon Mortimer by chance and thought she could use her skills." Palmer paused and took another mouthful of beer.

"So," he continued, "Simon Derwent went to The Beauty Centre to meet Cavendish but he actually met Mortimer. My guess is that Simon was not a bad looking guy, and now that we know the Mortimer's marriage wasn't stable, I'd put money on Sharon Mortimer being up for some action. Anyway they must have got talking and no doubt Derwent found out that Mortimer's old man was an architect, and a damned good one." He paused for another mouthful of beer.

"Well, after a while they slept together. This was all a few years ago. Then the blackmail started. Sharon Mortimer knew that if she were exposed it would mean financial ruin for her, so she went along with Derwent's demands, even though they meant stealing her husband's work from under his nose."

"So where does that leave Cavendish in all this?"

"It doesn't. While Simon Derwent was shagging Mortimer, his older brother was continuing his affair with Sam Baker. After a while, the two of them started to scheme. Richard Derwent clearly knew about his brother's antics, and his problems. There were huge rows over the younger brother's debts. I think also that he and Sam Baker realised that they could obtain the growing business of The Beauty Centre for themselves."

"How?" Karen was looking keenly at her lover.

"Well, Cavendish only had one living relative, Sam Baker. It seemed highly likely that if Cavendish had made a will then she would leave her estate to her cousin. Actually I checked the wills out and she had made such a will, and you won't be surprised when I tell you it was witnessed in part by Richard Derwent himself." He paused for another mouthful of beer.

"Now, where was I? So Sam Baker, who was not in the romantic marriage many believed to be the case, schemed with Richard Derwent to get rich beyond their wildest dreams. The plan was that they would use Mortimer to carry on working at The Beauty Centre and they would cream off the profits. Anyway, just over sixteen months ago, Mortimer stole some secret documents from her husband, and inevitably they ended up in the hands of Derwent. A few weeks later Baker and Derwent landed the huge contract and went out to celebrate. Everything was going to plan. It was the night that Sam Baker and Richard Derwent decided to act out the first stage of their macabre plot. Derwent bought the first round of drinks. He added something to Cavendish's drink, and probably a mild hypnotic to John Baker's. I've checked with the restaurant. Sam Baker, or should I say Cavendish, as widely reported, did not start throwing up. Actually she fainted. Now, John Baker was far more of a respectable person than Derwent will ever be. He took it upon himself to take Cavendish home. After all, apart from the others in the party, he was the only person who knew it was not his wife who was ill. Everyone assumed it was, simply because he took her home. Earlier that day Baker and Cavendish had been shopping and for a laugh had bought identical handbags. That was Sam Baker's doing, and sometime during the evening she swapped them over." Palmer paused. He drained the beer and looked up at his enraptured colleagues.

"Another drink, anyone." The heads were nodded in confirmation.

Five minutes later Palmer continued with the story.

"So John Baker and the virtually unconscious Cavendish climbed into the BMW with Derwent promising to drop Sam Baker off later on. As Baker drove off whatever was in his drink started to act. For whatever reason the car crashed and we know the rest. That left Sam Baker with her cousin's keys and her lover. What more natural than to spend the night together celebrating the completion of the first stage of their evil plan. Naturally, with the striking similarity between the two women and the switched identities the police assumed it was man and wife killed in the car. The cousin was the only living relative and with Derwent conveniently able to identify his dead partner it looked like they had everything sown up. They laid low for a few weeks until after the funerals and the wills had been read and so forth. Then Sam Baker reappeared on the scene as Cavendish.

She went to see Mortimer to check up on the business and probably told Mortimer that she was going to be less involved now as she had other interests she was pursuing. I don't think Mortimer liked the idea much, but she had no choice. I think, though I'm not sure, that Baker actually saw Simon Derwent at the shop at this point. Anyway she wasn't happy that her lover's brother was linked to the shop in any way – it would make things messy."

Palmer paused to rub his chin and look round at the still empty pub.

"Now there is one other thing you need to know about our Mrs. Baker. She had a rough ride at university, quite literally. Richard Derwent told me the story himself. She got mixed up in a group of trainee law students and ended up in a gang-bang in the back of a van one night. Afterwards she vowed to get her own back, no matter how long it took. Well, she'd started that a few years ago. The first two of the five men involved had been publicly disgraced. Then she'd located Goodland and Nash. They were going to be her next two victims, and it was convenient that they had started work for the same firm. So now, not only her greed, but also her personal desire for revenge, was working in her heart.

Richard Derwent was not worried about his brother's relationship with Mortimer in the same way that Baker was, so she went to visit Simon Derwent. She knew he only knew her as the wealthy partner of The Beauty Centre, Helen Cavendish. She also knew he was desperate and needed money, so she offered him some. In return he had to introduce her to some rather unsavoury characters. This he did and she set about putting into practice her plans to get rid of Goodland and Nash.

Part of that plan was to let slip the suggestion to Simon Derwent that she, in the assumed role of Cavendish, had killed the Bakers. She knew that Derwent did not like her and the hope was that Derwent would pass on the information, which he did. The timing was just right for her purposes. Baker, as Cavendish, made up her ridiculous story about not having any recollection about the night of the tragedy by transposing real events by a day, knowing that any half-witted investigator would sort it out for her. Then, her story firm in her mind she went to see Goodland. She even let Simon Derwent know the name of her solicitor. Not only that but two thugs were also given the relevant information." Palmer paused again and looked round.

"So, we come to the last few days. She waited until she was sure the police wanted to arrest her. Then, in a flurry of covert action she arranged to see Goodland. They'd only met a couple of times before, and he knew the past that she had told him. Obviously he didn't recognise her as the young woman he'd gang-raped several years ago. She asked him to get her an alibi, and at the same time she had hired people to see what happened next.

Goodland, as we know, contacted me and set the investigation in motion. What happened next isn't quite clear, but I'm pretty confident that their carefully arranged meeting away from the office wasn't quite as secret as she made out. I think that after she left the rendezvous he was picked up by two thugs, driven south and after a while thrown off the cliffs just outside Hastings.

As for the rest, Cavendish paid to have me followed. It worried her that I might dig too deeply and discover the real truth so I had to be warned off. My trip up to London to visit an old friend was a mistake, resulting in some needless cruelty, but it gave her hired thugs the opportunity to scare me off. That was where Miss. Cavendish, or should I say Mrs. Baker, got the psychology wrong. That incident made me more determined than before to get to the bottom of the matter. It was possibly Cavendish's, sorry Baker's first major error." Palmer stopped for another drink of beer. His colleagues watched and listened with growing interest.

"Now, she knew she'd be arrested. It was part of her plan, and she knew she'd end up on bail. She also knew that Nash would take over the case. Meantime, at some point over the past few weeks, Baker discovered that Sharon Mortimer had been to see her lover, Richard Derwent. I think she probably panicked herself into thinking they were having an affair. Actually, Mortimer went to try to get some money for Simon Derwent. The other Derwent told her that she'd have to provide some more secrets or something first. I worked that out from talking to a few people, so I set up Robert Mortimer with a plot. Unfortunately, the same evening that Sharon Mortimer stole the supposed secrets, Cavendish, sorry Sam Baker had plans of her own. She had decided that she needed to find out the truth about Mortimer. She visited Simon Derwent under some pretext or other and got talking to him about Mortimer. Unfortunately for Mortimer, while Baker was there she contacted Derwent to tell him she had the plans. It was an opportunity not to be missed. Cavendish, sorry Baker, told Simon Derwent that Sharon Mortimer was about to dispense with him as the middle guy, thus cutting off his source of income. Instead she was going to go straight to his older brother. It was a lie, but my guess is that Derwent needed drugs badly and his mind was more than a bit confused. Baker went and hid herself away when Mortimer arrived. The scene was probably ugly, and I imagine it ended with Simon Derwent beating Mortimer to death, probably accidentally." Palmer paused again as his colleagues swallowed the story he was feeding them.

"What wasn't accidental was what happened next. Eddie you saw it, though you probably didn't realise it."

"I did?" Eddie looked almost mesmerised.

"Yeah. When she left Simon Derwent's she took out her mobile phone and phoned one of her contacts. Simon Derwent had become expendable, and even a liability with Mortimer dead. She didn't know exactly what he knew, and with his drug crazed mind he could have made up all sorts of stories. Actually, I think she probably contacted some of his creditors. You saw them arrive, go in and come out. That's pretty much how long it took to finish him off."

"Yuck," Karen had turned somewhat pale.

"Sorry love, but that's the reality of what happens if you can't pay for your habit. There isn't much leeway. So Baker and Derwent's master plan is beginning to fall apart and she can no longer be sure he doesn't have other lovers. She goes down to his country pad and spends a final night with him. At some point the guys who killed the other Derwent drop by to get paid for their work. Next day Cavendish, or rather Baker, fails to show at her solicitors. Not a surprise. The plan has changed. She now has to leave the country, but first she has some unfinished business to attend to.

Whilst talking to her new solicitor, Nash, I realised he was part of the gang that had raped

262

Baker. I then had to find Baker and fast. It took half the morning to check her flat and find that she'd gone. It seemed likely she'd gone back to the country pad of Richard Derwent. She had, but had already left, probably with him in his vehicle. I didn't think she was such a thorough woman, but while I was there one of her thugs came and took her Fiesta away, probably to destroy it by torching it. It was when that happened the penny really dropped. She was leaving, for good, only I didn't think Richard Derwent was now still part of her plans.

She's a resourceful woman, and despite their little fracas a couple of nights earlier over her paranoia about him seeing another woman, he still fancied her. So he took her to the airport. It was, as far as he was concerned, a short trip away until everything had calmed down. So far as she was concerned, it was a new start." Palmer again paused for a mouthful of ale.

"At the airport she feigned fear at being followed, so he went to get the ticket. While he did so, she pulled a little package out of her suitcase, primed it and put it in the glove compartment. There could be no one who knew her real identity left alive now. She was leaving the country as Mrs. Baker, only to materialise somewhere else as someone completely different. We may never know." Palmer sipped some more beer, relishing the moment.

"Now, she did not know how close I was getting to her. And she did not know how much help I could get hold of. The guys at the airport were really useful as was Eddie. So far as she was concerned, once Derwent came back with the ticket she was away free and he was a dead man. Even though she had reluctantly had to forego getting even with Nash. When she got arrested and Nash had turned up it gave her one last chance. It was a desperate attempt from a now desperate and scheming woman. The rest we all know.

One final thing, Karen, it was when you mentioned a switch at the restaurant, that I began to see the light in this case. That's the second time your pictures have been so helpful. Thanks, darling." He reached over and kissed her tenderly.

The End

Get Damien's next case "Rite of Death" at https://fiction4all.com